William Harrison Ainsworth

John Law

Vol. 3

SALZWASSER
VERLAG

William Harrison Ainsworth

John Law

Vol. 3

Reprint of the original, first published in 1864.

1st Edition 2022 | ISBN: 978-3-75259-409-6

Verlag (Publisher): Salzwasser Verlag GmbH, Zeilweg 44, 60439 Frankfurt, Deutschland
Vertretungsberechtigt (Authorized to represent): E. Roepke, Zeilweg 44, 60439 Frankfurt, Deutschland
Druck (Print): Books on Demand GmbH, In de Tarpen 42, 22848 Norderstedt, Deutschland

JOHN LAW

THE PROJECTOR.

BY

WILLIAM HARRISON AINSWORTH.

IN THREE VOLUMES.

VOL. III.

CONTENTS OF VOL. III.

BOOK V.—*continued.*

LA RUE QUINCAMPOIX.

BOOK VI.

THE COMPTROLLER-GENERAL

BOOK VII.

THE COMTE DE HORN.

BOOK VIII.

THE DOWNFAL OF THE SYSTEM.

BOOK V.

(CONTINUED.)

LA RUE QUINCAMPOIX.

IX.

ROOKS AND PIGEONS.

PEACE being thus restored, the two Irishmen, who had retired to the back of the room, came forward, and made their best bows to the company, but in such a grotesque style as to excite the laughter of all those who beheld them.

"Who the deuce are these originals?" asked De Mille of Evelyn. "They appear to be countrymen of yours."

"I have no sort of acquaintance with them," replied Evelyn. "They look like parvenus. May I venture to ask your names, gentlemen?" he added to the Irishmen. "If I am not mistaken, you are both from the Sister Isle?"

"Yer hon'r is right," replied Sir Terence. "This jontleman is Sir Patrick Molloy, and I am Sir Terence O'Flaherty, at yer hon'r's sarvice. Mighty glad we are to meet wid a fellow-countryman on an occasion like the present, and greatly obleeged we are to yer hon'r, as well as to the rest of the hon'r'ble company, for affordin' us an asylum. If we might make so bould, we should be delighted to prove our gratitude by trating the company to a glass of wine."

Evelyn having communicated Sir Terence's wishes to the others, De Mille at once called out,

"Accept his offer by all means. Something may be done with these fools," he added, in an under tone, to De Horn.

"You think so?" said De Horn.

"I'm sure of it," replied the other. And, going to the door, he opened it, and called out, "Hola, mon hôte!—Rossignol, I say!"

"Voilà, messieurs, voilà," replied the cabaretier, instantly making his appearance.

"Here is the host," observed Evelyn to Sir Terence. "What orders do you desire to give him?"

"Bid him bring half a dozen of the best wine his house can furnish," replied the Irishman.

This order being conveyed to Rossignol, he observed,

"Is the gentleman aware that the best vin de Bordeaux costs fifty livres a bottle?"

On this being made known to Sir Terence, he called out, angrily,

"Wot's that he says?—fifty livres a bottle! By the powers! it ought to be good at the price. But what d'ye stand starin' at, ye ugly spalpeen?" he added to Rossignol, who of course did not comprehend a word he said. "Be off, and fetch the wine. Divil take you! do you think I can't pay for it?" But finding that the host did not move, he produced a bulky porte-feuille, from which he took a note, calling out, as he flourished it before Rossignol's eyes, "Here's a billy for five thousand livres. Will that pay you?"

"A l'instant, monsieur — à l'instant!" cried the host, disappearing.

"I thought the rascal would understand what this meant," observed Sir Terence, with a laugh, as he replaced the note in his porte-feuille.

"Bedad! I hope I haven't lost my pocket-book in the scrimmage," cried Sir Patrick. "No, it's here safe enough," he added, taking it out and examining it.

"Both these boobies have well-filled porte-feuilles," remarked De Mille to the Comte de Horn. "We must contrive to empty them."

"Sur ma foi, fortune seems to have thrown them in our way," rejoined De Horn, in the same tone. "What a pity it is they can't speak French."

"Oh, they can talk well enough for our purpose," said De Mille. "Besides, M. Harcourt will act as interpreter."

"With so much money about you as you appear to have, gentlemen," observed Evelyn to the two Irishmen, "you ought to avoid getting into brawls. There are plenty of cut-purses in the crowd, and it is well you have not got your pockets picked."

"By the powers! we must be more careful in future," said Sir Terence. "Divil a bit did we mane to git into a row at all, but was goin' about like paiceable folk, meddlin' wi' no man, when our English broker comes up to us, and, says he, 'I'll bring you to a customer who'll sell you some shares.' So we pushes our way through the crowd, until we comes right opposite to this tavern, and there, sure enough, we finds our customer standin' beside the little hunchback — Teebow they calls him, though he ain't much of a beau — who lets out his hump as a writin'-desk to the Mississippians. Well, a bargain was struck, and our broker was jist makin' a note of the transaction on little Teebow's back, when up comes two or three tall swaggerin' fellows, and without sayin' by yer lave, knocks him and the dwarf over togither. This makes the saucy blades laugh heartily, but Pat and I soon stops their fun, for quick as lightnin' we brings down our sticks on their showlders—whack!—whack! 'How d'ye like it?' says I, givin' the fellow nearest me a smart crack on the crown. 'That'll tache ye manners next time.' Well, he didn't seem to like it at all, but grinned like a bah-boon, and began to saacre and swear like a trooper. So I gives him another gentle tap on the sconce, but instead of pacifyin' him, it makes him swear like ten thousand divils just let loose. Out flies his toastin'-fork, and he would have spitted me in a trice if I hadn't bin too sharp for him, and made him drop his weep'n. Jist then Sir Patrick roars out for help, and, turnin' round, I finds him hard pressed by three or four ruffians. 'Och, murder, my jewel!' cries I, 'I'll be with you in a jiffy.' So I lays about me right and left like a thrasher, and soon clears a way to Sir Patrick; and then we stands back to back, and bids defiance to the whole host ov 'em. However, with sich odds against us we must soon have got the worst ov it, if we hadn't found shelter here —thanks be to yer hon'r and the noble company. Ah, here comes the wine."

As he spoke, Rossignol made his appearance, followed by a garçon bearing the wine.

The table was then quickly cleared by the active host and his equally active attendant of the empty flasks and the débris of the déjeûner. Fresh glasses were brought, and a couple of corks drawn. The wine was then tasted by Sir Terence, who smacked his lips over it and pronounced it excellent, and he then proceeded to fill to the brim all the glasses of the company, bowing to each as he fulfilled his task. After raising the glass to his lips, but without drinking a drop, Cossard rose, and, apologising for retiring, quitted the room. Evelyn was about to follow his example, but De Mille begged him to stay a few moments, saying,

"It you leave us, M. Harcourt, we shan't be able to converse with our new friends."

The Irishmen also besought him so earnestly to remain, that he could not refuse compliance. However, not all the entreaties of Sir Terence could induce him to empty his glass. De Mille and the others, who were of far less temperate habits, showed no such reluctance, but drank as freely as the Irishmen themselves, and, in a very short space of time, four out of the six bottles were emptied. Conversation was carried on between the Irishmen and the others through the medium of Evelyn, who good-naturedly consented to act as interpreter, and as the generous wine loosened the tongue of Sir Terence, who was the chief speaker, he became more and more communicative, detailed the interview which he and Sir Patrick had had with the great Mr. Law, boasted of their gilt coach and footmen, and invited all the company to visit them at the Hôtel de la Régence, in the Rue Saint Honoré.

"Be good enough to tell the gentlemen, M. Harcourt," said De Mille, glancing, as he spoke, expressively at the two Irishmen, "that the Comte de Horn, the Chevalier D'Etampes, and myself, Captain de Mille, are enchanted to make their acquaintance—say 'enchanted,' if you please, M. Harcourt. Add, that we shall do ourselves the honour of calling upon them at their hotel, and shall always be delighted—pray say 'delighted,' M. Harcourt—to see them at the Hôtel de Flandre. Do not omit to say that we are infinitely obliged—'infinitely,' if you please, M. Harcourt—by their proposal to lend us their carriage, and we shall not hesitate to avail ourselves of their polite offer."

When this was conveyed to the two Irishmen by Evelyn, they both arose and bowed with ludicrous ceremoniousness to De Mille and the others, who, in order to humour the jest, rose likewise, and bowed with mock formality in return.

"I am ashamed to put you to so much trouble, M. Harcourt," said De Mille, apologetically, "but my disgraceful ignorance of your language leaves me no alternative. We all come to the Rue Quincampoix with one object, namely, to buy or sell shares. Will you ask our new friends whether they are disposed to sell or buy? I can meet them in either way."

This question being put by Evelyn, Sir Terence immediately replied,

"Bedad, I'm always ready for bis'ness. Ask the capt'n if he has any 'daughters' and 'granddaughters' for sale."

Whereunto, on the question being propounded to him, De Mille replied that he had ten *filles* and twice as many *petites filles*, for each of which he expected ten thousand livres.

"Jist the sort ov fam'ly I should like to possess. I'll take 'em at the price," replied Sir Terence, producing his big pocket-book, and counting out thirty billets de banque, each worth ten thousand livres. "But all these girls ought to have a 'mother' to take care of them," he added, with a laugh. "Has the capt'n got one? And, if so, wot's her valley?"

De Mille replied that he had a "mother"—more than one, indeed—as many as ten—but he could not part with them under twelve thousand livres —with a premium.

"The owld ladies stands higher in the market than their daughters, since they commands a premium," observed Sir Terence. "They're too dear for me."

"I'll take 'em, capt'n," said Sir Patrick, bring ing out his pocket-book, "and as many more as you like to sell."

As soon as this little transaction was concluded, a fresh bottle of wine was opened, and all the glasses, except Evelyn's, replenished.

"Permit me, jontlemen, to propose a toast," said Sir Terence, getting up, glass in hand. "As Sir Patrick and myself owes our fortins to Mr.

Law, we ought not to omit drinkin' his very good health on an occasion like the present. Here's Mr. Law! and long life to him!" he added, draining his glass to the last drop.

"Mr. Law, and long life to him!" cried Sir Patrick, following his example.

"A la santé de Monseigneur Law!" cried the others, enthusiastically.

"I cannot refuse that toast," said Evelyn, filling his glass. "Long live Mr. Law! and may he long occupy the proud position he has attained!" And he added, "Are you aware, gentlemen, that he is about to visit the Rue Quincampoix to-day?"

"You don't say so?" exclaimed De Mille. "I have heard nothing about it. At what hour is he likely to be here?"

"That I cannot inform you," replied Evelyn. "I have heard, on pretty good authority, that the young king and the Regent are likewise coming here to-day, and if so, Mr. Law will naturally be in attendance upon his majesty."

"Are you sure you are correctly informed, sir?" remarked the Comte de Horn. "I supped with the Regent last night at the Palais Royal, and nothing was said about this royal visit."

"I believe my information will prove to be correct, M. le Comte, though I am not at liberty to mention the source from which I obtained it," replied Evelyn. "No public intimation has been given of the intended royal visit, and for this reason—his youthful majesty desires to see the street as it is—thronged with Mississippians. All its peculiar features would be lost if business were interrupted."

"Very true," observed De Horn; "the Rue Quincampoix would be like any other crowded street if it wanted its extraordinary bustle and animation. But I don't think that even the young king's presence would stop the stock-jobbing, when at its height. What say you, De Mille?"

"I am quite of your opinion," replied the person appealed to. "Men won't throw away the chance of making a million for the pleasure of looking at a boy-monarch. He comes to see *them* —they have something better to do than to waste their time in staring at him."

"If his youthful majesty should see the crowd in a state of excitement," remarked D'Etampes, "he will fancy all his subjects are gone mad."

"And he won't be far out if he does think so," said Evelyn, with a laugh.

"Well, we are all as mad as the rest," cried De Mille; "and for my part, I have no wish to regain my senses. But will you do me the favour to ask our new friends if they would like a game at quadrille, a party at piquet, or a little hazard? Hola! Rossignol!" he shouted. "Cards and dice, dy'e hear!"

"De suite, monsieur, de suite!" responded the host; and he presently appeared with half a dozen packs of cards and a couple of dice-boxes, which he placed on the table beside De Mille.

"Will you play, gentlemen?" cried De Mille.

"Shall it be this?—or this?" he added, suiting the action to the word, and alternately touching the cards and dice-boxes.

As the invitation could not be misunderstood, Sir Terence immediately arose, and taking up a pack of cards, said, "This."

"Very good," replied De Mille, with a smile. "The language of gaming is fortunately intelligible to all the world. Shall we play piquet?"

"Piquet, by all manes, capt'n," replied Sir Terence, pleased with his own cleverness. "We both ov us understands that game, havin' often played it at the Cheerman's Club at the Blue Posts."

"I advise you not to play now," said Evelyn. "If you do, you'll lose your money. You are no match for these gentlemen."

"Poh! poh! we're not sich greenhorns as that, are we, Sir Patrick?" cried Sir Terence. "Now that we belongs to the quality, we must do as the quality does."

"Tell the gentlemen we play for nothing under five thousand livres," said De Mille to Harcourt.

"What was that observation about livres?" inquired Sir Terence.

Evelyn told him, and added, "I must repeat my caution to you."

But Sir Terence only laughed, and said, "Oh! we're not afeared. We like a little gamblin'. Hitherto we've had good luck, but if it should desert us, we shan't feel the loss of a few thousand livres—eh, Sir Patrick?"

"Not we," replied the personage addressed, bringing out his porte-feuille, the sight of which excited the cupidity of De Mille and his companions, and they resolved to empty it before they parted with him. "We can easily make up our losses before we laves the street."

"Again, I say be upon your guard," remarked Evelyn to the Irishmen. "I more than suspect the persons you are about to play with are rooks."

"Rooks did you say?" cried Sir Terence.

"Then iv they takes us for pigeons, they'll find us deuced hard to pluck. Sir Patrick and I are both wide awake, and can see as far into a millstone as most folk, so we shall be up to their tricks."

"Ay, and down upon 'em, too, if they attempt any foul play," said Sir Patrick.

"If you're wise, you'll come with me," said Evelyn, preparing to depart.

"Won't you stay and take a hand with us, M. Harcourt?" said De Mille, who was engaged in removing all the deuces, trays, fours and fives from a pack of cards, preparatory to commencing the game.

"I never play," replied Evelyn.

"Never play! You surprise me," cried De Mille. "Then you don't know the greatest pleasure in life."

"Always excepting stock-jobbing, which I hold to be more exciting than cards," said De Horn.

"Stock-jobbing *is* gambling," said De Mille.

"So M. Harcourt is wrong in asserting that he never plays."

"At all events, I never meddle with cards and dice," said Evelyn.

"Well, stop a few minutes, I beg of you, if only to explain matters to your countrymen," observed De Mille. "We should be sorry to take any advantage of them."

"I can be of no further assistance," said Evelyn. "So I must leave them in your hands."

"And be assured we'll take every care of them," said De Horn.

"I don't doubt it," replied Evelyn.

And with a warning look at the Irishmen, which, however, was quite lost upon them, he quitted the room.

X.

A FEW GROUPS IN THE RUE QUINCAMPOIX.

A STEP from the tavern into the crowded street was like a plunge into a torrent. Finding it in vain to struggle against the stream, which was now flowing towards the Rue Aubry le Boucher, Evelyn suffered himself to be borne in that direction. Before long, however, a check was experienced, and all circulation was for a short time impeded. With some difficulty, Evelyn managed to extricate himself from the throng, and sought refuge in the open doorway of a house, from which position he was able to survey the tumultuous scene.

An extraordinary sight it was, and though Evelyn had often witnessed it before, it had still as much interest for him as ever. The crowd in the Rue Quincampoix was like no other crowd. Never before had such a motley assemblage been brought together—nor ever will be again. Such was the variety of costumes and characters that the scene resembled a grand carnival, except that the majority of the actors came for purposes of speculation, and not for amusement.

Where, but in the Rue Quincampoix, could have been seen nobles and manants, priests and valets, magistrates, philosophers, and chevaliers d'industrie, bargaining together? Where, but in this street could be seen richly-attired women of high rank, and of great beauty, mingling with such a crowd, and transacting business with any one they met? Nothing but the frenzy for gain which had seized persons of all classes could account for such proceedings. The wonderful fortunes known to have been made in the Rue Quincampoix caused every one to rush there, hoping to be equally lucky. Business was universally neglected. Nothing was thought of but stock-jobbing. Nothing talked of but the price of actions—how they rose—how they fell. Even in our speculating times it is scarcely possible to form a notion of the frenzy which then prevailed—which spread like a contagion through Paris—through all the provinces of France, and, indeed, throughout Europe. In a satirical carol of the day we read of

Les plaisans viremens
Et continuels changemens
Que l'on a vu dans le royaume
De Quincampoix et de Vendôme,
Ou l'achat et le dividend
Causoient un rumeur si grande,
Qu'on ne vit jamais tant de rats
Obséder gens de tous états;
Mari, femme, garçon, et fille,
Laquais, servantes, la famille
En un mot, sans rien excepter,
Venit jouer et blanquetter.
Là de tous pays et provinces,

Marchands, magistrats, artisans,
Prélats, guerriers, et courtisans,
Ducs et pairs, même des princes,
Non du pays, mais bien forains,
Accouroient comme des essaims,
Malgré vent, grèle, pluie, et crotte,
Pour y jouer à la marotte,
En beaux et bons deniers comptans,
Contre les voleurs calotines,
Dont la France et terres voisines
Se pourront souvenir long temps.

We may judge of the frenzy that prevailed, when we see that it made the haughtiest aristocrats lose all respect for themselves, and that while under the influence of this fever they stooped to practices from which in calmer moments they would have revolted. But if we censure princes, peers, and other exalted personages for conduct so unworthy of their station, what shall we say of noble dames who could so far forget themselves as to figure in such a scene? Yet, as we have shown, women of the highest rank constantly frequented the Rue Quincampoix, and were amongst the most eager jobbers. Utterly disregarding the construction that might be put upon their conduct, heedless of the annoyances and inconveniences to which they were subjected, equally heedless of the familiarity with which they were treated, without a blush at the ribaldry and licentious discourse that constantly met their ears, they went on through the throng, carrying on their speculations whenever a chance offered. It was noticeable that these high-born dames, and, indeed, ladies generally, declined to deal with each other, and invariably carried on their transactions with those of the opposite sex, no matter of what rank—lacquey, artisan, peasant, petit-maître, or peer—over whom they deemed their charms might give them an advantage.

From the position which he had just gained, Evelyn looked around on this strange scene. Everybody seemed in a state of the wildest excitement. A sudden rise had taken place, and buyers and sellers were equally clamorous. The din was prodigious, almost bewildering, and would have stunned any one unaccustomed to it. But those who were in the thickest of the crowd, and engaged in the uproar, knew very well what was said. Transactions for large sums were carried on with astonishing rapidity. *Mères*, *filles*, and *petites filles*, were dealt out with one hand, and billets de banque received with the other. The countenances of those engaged in these rapidly-conducted operations were a study, and could they have been seized at the moment, would have formed an unequalled picture.

As he ran his eye rapidly over the throng, several groups attracted Evelyn's attention. One was composed of a lady richly dressed, and evidently of rare personal attractions, though her features were partially concealed by a half mask of black velvet. She was buying actions from two brokers, for which she paid a considerable sum in billets de banque, and in the excitement of the transaction her mask fell off, and disclosed the dark eyes, dark tresses, and charming countenance of the Regent's *petit corbeau noir*, the Comtesse de Parabère. The mask was quickly replaced, and the countess disappeared as quickly as she could.

The next lady upon whom our observer's eye rested was a person of very inferior condition, and with but little pretension to personal attraction, though she, too, was very richly dressed. As she wore no mask, Evelyn, to whom she had been previously pointed out, and who was acquainted with her history, instantly recognised her as Madame Chaumont, a widow who had come to Paris about a lawsuit, and who had already gained a hundred millions by her speculations in this street. She was surrounded by Mississippians, with all of whom she appeared to be dealing.

Not far from the lucky Madame Chaumont stood the Prince de Conti, who was now as regularly to be seen in the Rue Quincampoix as any other jobber. At this moment the prince was selling shares to a stout, well-looking man, whose countenance, though he could not recal it, was familiar to Evelyn. This stout personage was no other than Law's ci-devant coachman, Hippolyte.

The next person to attract Evelyn's notice was M. Chirac, the Regent's principal physician, a man ordinarily of grave exterior and extremely dignified deportment, but he now appeared to be in a state of great excitement, and was gesticulating furiously to M. Chambéry, a speculator with whom he was dealing. Like Madame Chaumont, Chambéry was a singular instance of the caprice of fortune. A poor Savoyard, he gained a bare livelihood by acting as a commissioner, but since the commencement of the System he had contrived to amass forty millions, and at this particular juncture he was endeavouring to purchase an office in the royal household.

Close to Chambéry, and now availing himself of the broad omoplate of Martial to jot down his calculations, was Vincent Leblanc, another speculator, who had profited to the extent of many millions by the System. The two persons with whom Leblanc was now transacting business were no other than Montesquieu and Fontenelle. These two celebrated men were kept in countenance by a pair of the ripest scholars of the day—namely, the Abbé Terrason and M. de la Mothe.

Many other remarkable personages came under Evelyn's ken. Among the throng he recognised three of the Regent's Roués, De Broglie, Brancas, and Nocé, and in the balcony of a house on the opposite side of the street he discovered the Duchesse de Brissac, the beautiful Marquise de Bellefonds, Madame de Blanchefort, and Mademoiselles d'Espinoy and De Melun. In fact, almost every window in this part of the street was garnished with charming court dames. The ladies, as we have previously intimated, were by no means indifferent spectatresses of the scene, but took a prominent part in the extraordinary drama going on, being constantly engaged in speculations with the Mississippians and brokers in the street.

A striking feature in the crowd was the number of richly-dressed persons, and these were by no means people of the highest rank, for those who made money invariably expended it in costly stuffs, and clothed themselves in embroidered velvets and silks, and even in cloth of gold, wearing buttons of solid gold and silver. This extravagance was carried to such a point that all the warehouses in the Rue St. Honoré were emptied of their stores of silks, velvets, tissues, lace, and embroidery, and it was found necessary to check the over-indulgence in rich stuffs by a sumptuary law.

On the present occasion a laughable incident occurred. A Mississippian of the lower order, but who was arrayed in a blue velvet coat bedizened with gold lace, and furnished with buttons of solid gold, deliberately took it off, and gave it to a broker with whom he was bargaining to make up the amount of a share. But he undertook to redeem the pledge within five minutes, and so expeditiously were operations conducted that he got back his coat within the given time.

Strange indeed was the manner in which the transactions were conducted. The brokers refused nothing but specie. A young, beautiful, and richly-dressed woman, having no other means of obtaining the shares she coveted, gave all her jewels to a broker. One man paid for a few shares with his title-deeds, and deemed himself singularly fortunate. Another offered a mortgage deed, and a third bills of exchange. Mistakes were occasionally made, and a priest in his hurry to conclude a bargain handed over a billet d'enterrement instead of a billet de banque.

Laughable encounters constantly took place. Husbands, who thought their wives safe at home, discovered them in the crowd; servants, who ought to have been engaged in their household duties, stumbled upon their masters or mistresses; clerks confronted their employers; and debtors could not avoid their creditors.

But these encounters, and many others of a similar nature, rarely led to unpleasant consequences. People were too much engrossed by the business they came upon to squabble. Thus the husband passed on without stopping to upbraid his wife; the clerk escaped unquestioned; and the servant was excused. Amongst the crowd Evelyn descried several persons who had profited enormously by the System—to wit, old Samuel Bernard, the banker; Antoine Crozat, of whom mention has been previously made; M. Fargès, originally a common soldier, and now worth twenty millions; the Sieur André, who had made sixty millions; and Messieurs Le Blanc and De la Faye, each of whom had made eighteen millions.

Evelyn had just completed his survey of the various groups we have described, when a tall, stately-looking valet, in a rich livery, made his way towards him. It was Thierry.

"Lady Catherine Law is in the house on the other side of the street, immediately opposite to where you stand, sir," said Thierry, "and having observed you among the crowd, she has sent me to say she will be glad to see you. I may add," he continued, in a low tone, "that his majesty is expected in a few minutes. If it will please you to follow me I will conduct you to her ladyship."

It is scarcely necessary to say that Evelyn gladly accepted the invitation, and was soon across the street with his conductor.

XI.

OF THE OVATION RECEIVED BY LAW.

THE house to which he was taken was the largest in the Rue Quincampoix, and was not without some pretensions to architectural beauty. It stood back a little from the street, and possessed handsome windows and elaborately-wrought iron balconies.

The door was guarded by soldiers, but at a word from Thierry they allowed Evelyn to pass, and he entered the house with his conductor.

The guard at the door proving conclusively that some persons of importance must be inside the house which Evelyn had just entered, the general gaze was directed towards the windows, but for some time the public curiosity remained ungratified.

At length, a party of richly-dressed ladies appeared at the upper windows, and some of them, in order to obtain a better view of the street, came forward into the balconies. Among the foremost of these was Lady Catherine Law, who, being recognised by the assemblage, was enthusiastically cheered. With Lady Catherine, besides her children, were Colombe and Belinda.

It being now certain that Law must be in the house, loud shouts were raised for him by the crowd, but, as he did not respond to the calls, they increased in vehemence, until the whole street became in an uproar. The cries were so loud and persistent, that at length Law yielded, and stepped forth upon the balcony on the first floor, which had hitherto remained unoccupied, and bowed to the assemblage.

On his appearance the most frantic demonstrations of enthusiasm and delight were made, and the tremendous shout which arose was carried along to either extremity of the Rue Quincampoix, and was caught up by the crowds in all the adjacent streets.

It being evident from Law's manner that he desired to address the assemblage, silence was at length obtained, and in a brief speech, which, being uttered in a clear and sonorous voice, was heard to a considerable distance, he thanked them for the gratifying reception they had given him, assuring them it was ample reward for all his exertions to improve the finances of the kingdom, and extend its commerce.

"My aim," he said, in conclusion, "has been to relieve the state from debt, to free the people from vexatious imposts, and to render trade flourishing, and I am proud to think I have succeeded."

"You have!—you have!" cried a thousand voices. "You are the preserver of the country—

the benefactor of the people. We are indebted to you, and to you alone, for our present prosperity. You have made us all rich and happy. Poverty and misery are no longer known in France. Vive Monseigneur Law!"

Never before had Law experienced such emotions as now swelled within his breast. Fully believing that he had conferred incalculable benefits upon the country, believing also that his System would endure, he accepted the homage paid him as if his due, and exulted in his triumph.

His appearance at that moment excited universal admiration. His lofty and imposing figure, his strikingly handsome lineaments, his dignified deportment—all contributed to the effect he produced. So wonderful was the enthusiasm of the assemblage, that it seemed as if they would never leave off shouting. Law bowed to them repeatedly, and whenever he did so the acclamations were renewed.

"Messieurs!" he said, as soon as the vociferations had in some degree subsided, "you have already bestowed more praise upon me than I deserve. Your cheers must now be addressed to one to whom they are rightfully due. To arouse the spirit of loyalty which I am certain burns in every breast, I have only to mention that your young king is present."

No sooner was this announcement made than fresh acclamations arose, and shouts resounded on all sides of "Vive le Roi."

In the midst of these loyal demonstrations Law bowed and withdrew, and presently afterwards, in compliance with the wishes of his subjects, the young king came out upon the balcony. His habiliments, of light blue satin, set off his graceful figure to the utmost advantage. He was attended by the Regent and the Duc de Bourbon, and behind him stood the Maréchal de Villeroi and Law.

The young monarch's appearance was the signal for fresh demonstrations of loyalty and devotion;

but the enthusiasm of the assemblage was roused to the highest pitch when Law was called forward by the king, who addressed a few words to him, the import of which could easily be conjectured by those who witnessed the scene.

But if any doubt could have remained, it was dispelled by the Regent, who called out with a loud voice,

"Messieurs! his majesty desires publicly to thank M. Law for the important services he has rendered to the state and to the country at large!"

On this, the plaudits were louder than ever, and the whole place resounded with shouts of "Vivent le Roi et Monseigneur Law!"

XII.

WHAT PASSED BETWEEN THE YOUNG KING AND MADEMOISELLE LAW.

BOWING graciously to the assemblage, and giving his hand to his uncle, who stood close behind him, the young monarch withdrew from the balcony.

"I hope your majesty does not regret the visit you have paid to the Rue Quincampoix?" observed the Regent, as he conducted his royal nephew to a fauteuil.

"On the contrary, I have been greatly interested by all I have seen and heard," replied Louis.

"Until this moment I had no conception how very highly M. Law is esteemed by the people. What can be done to mark our sense of the services he has rendered to the kingdom?"

"I would recommend your majesty to begin by placing the entire administration of the finances in his hands," returned the Regent.

"I wish to do so," said Louis. "But I understand from the Maréchal de Villeroi that he is disqualified from holding the office of comptroller-general."

"The disqualifications may be removed, sire," returned the Regent. "I trust M. Law may be induced by the arguments of the Abbé Tencin, who has undertaken the task of his conversion, to renounce his heretical doctrines and embrace the faith of Rome. If so, the main difficulty will be obviated, since his naturalisation will follow as a matter of course."

"Your majesty will do well to reflect before promising the appointment," said Villeroi in the king's ear. "Wait to see how the System goes on."

"I am perfectly satisfied with what it has done already," replied Louis. "I hope the Abbé Tencin will fulfil his godly task, mon oncle," he added to the Regent. "In that case, M. Law shall have the post."

"I ought to inform your majesty," said the Regent, "that Lady Catherine Law, with her son and daughter, are in an upper room of this house. Will it please you to receive them?"

Louis graciously assented, and on being acquainted with his majesty's pleasure, Law quitted the room, and presently returned with Lady Catherine and his children, all of whom were presented by the Regent, and received with the greatest affability by the young king. To Lady Catherine, Louis spoke of the ovation her husband had just received from the public. To Mademoiselle Law he addressed some compliments which she could not fail to appreciate. And he gratified young John Law immensely by telling him he was the very image of his father.

"Pray stay a moment, mademoiselle," he added to Kate Law, who was about to retire. "I want to say a word to you about my ball. I hope you like dancing?"

"I am passionately fond of it, sire," she replied.

"I fancied so," he said. "We will dance a minuet together—unless you prefer any other figure."

"The minuet is my favourite dance, sire," replied Kate.

"I am glad to hear it," said Louis, smiling. "But I am arranging a little ballet in which you and your brother must take part."

"Excuse me, sire, for reminding you that the ballet is already filled up," remarked Villeroi.

"Who has filled it up?" demanded Louis, noticing Kate's look of disappointment.

"I have, sire," replied the maréchal, "with young persons qualified by their rank to dance with your majesty."

"You have taken too much upon yourself, M. le Maréchal, in making this arrangement without my sanction," said Louis, "and you will have to undo your work. Two of those whom you have selected must be left out, and their places assigned to Mademoiselle Law and her brother."

"I hope your majesty will not insist upon this," remonstrated Villeroi. "It will embarrass me greatly."

"I cannot help that," said Louis.

"Oh! pray, sire, do not let the arrangements be disturbed on my account!" said Kate. "It will be quite sufficient gratification to me to witness the ballet, without taking part in it."

"But you *shall* dance in it, mademoiselle, and so shall your brother," said Louis. "M. le Maréchal, you will take care that my injunctions are obeyed. Is there anything more that can be done to render the ball agreeable to you, mademoiselle?" he added to Kate.

"Oh! sire, you are too considerate," she cried.

"Not at all, mademoiselle," he rejoined. "As the daughter of one who has rendered such important services to the kingdom, you are entitled to every consideration from me. Is there any one whom you desire to have invited to the ball?"

"Can this be the great-grandson of the Grand Monarque?" mentally ejaculated Villeroi, with a groan.

"Your majesty emboldens me to mention that I have one friend whom I love as a sister—Mademoiselle Colombe Laborde—and it would indeed gratify me if she were honoured with an invitation."

"She shall have one," returned Louis. "Mark what I say, M. le Maréchal. Mademoiselle Colombe Laborde is to be invited."

"It shall be done, sire," groaned Villeroi.

"Mademoiselle Laborde is a very charming

person," observed the Regent. "But your majesty may judge of her yourself; for, unless I am mistaken, she is with Lady Catherine's party in the upper room. Shall she be presented?"

"By all means," replied Louis; "and let the whole of Lady Catherine Law's party be introduced at the same time."

This order being communicated by the Regent to a gentleman in waiting at the door, it was at once carried into effect, and shortly afterwards Belinda and her husband, Sir Harry Archer, the Earl of Islay, Lord Belhaven, Evelyn Harcourt, and Mademoiselle Laborde, were severally announced, and presented to the young king, by whom they were all very graciously received. Louis was particularly struck by Colombe, and told Kate he was much indebted to her for enabling him to have so charming a person at his ball.

The presentations being made without the usual form and ceremony, there was no restraint, and everybody was delighted with the affability displayed by the young king.

When Evelyn came up to make his obeisance to the youthful monarch, the Regent remarked to his royal nephew, "Sire, I am about to ask a favour of you."

"You can ask nothing that I will refuse, mon oncle," replied Louis, smiling. "What is it?"

"You have invited this young lady"—pointing to Colombe—"to please Mademoiselle Law. Invite this young gentleman"—indicating Evelyn—"to please me."

"With all my heart," rejoined the king. "Take care M. Harcourt is invited," he added to Villeroi.

"Your majesty had better invite all the company," said the old maréchal, unable to repress his vexation.

"An excellent suggestion!" exclaimed the Regent. "They are all M. Law's friends."

"And as such they are welcome to me," said

Louis. "I am obliged by the hint, M. le Maréchal, and will act upon it. Take care that all the company are invited."

The old maréchal looked perfectly aghast at the command, but did not venture to offer any remonstrance.

"See it be done," echoed the Regent, laughing at Villeroi's consternation. "Your majesty is quite right. Too much honour cannot be shown M. Law."

"And in honouring my friends, your majesty confers most honour upon me," said Law.

"These are but trifling favours, sir, and scarcely merit your thanks," said Louis. "We have better things in store for you. Have we not, mon oncle?"

"Ay, that we have," replied the Regent. "But enough for the present. Does your majesty desire to tarry here longer?"

"No," replied Louis. "I have had a surfeit of strange sights, and have no appetite for more.

Adieu, M. Law. I shall ever retain a pleasant recollection of my visit to the Rue Quincampoix."

He then arose, and taking the hand of the Regent, graciously saluted the company, who drew aside, and bent reverentially as he passed out.

His youthful majesty was followed by the Duc de Bourbon and Villeroi; and in this manner he was conducted to his carriage, which awaited him in the Rue Saint Denis, at the rear of the house.

End of the Fifth Book.

BOOK VI.

THE COMPTROLLER-GENERAL.

I.

THE REALISERS.

HITHERTO, great and unquestionable benefits had flowed to France from Law's System. Commerce had not only been revived, but was continually on the increase. The number of manufactures was prodigiously augmented. Evidences of general prosperity were proclaimed in a manner the most unmistakable—not only in the improvement of trade and commerce, but by the liquidation of debts, and the almost total cessation of failures. Great public works were commenced.

Splendid hotels and maisons de plaisance were built. Barracks were for the first time constructed; the Pont de Blois was built; and the Canal de Bourgogne planned. Some of the noblest buildings of Paris date from Law's epoch. During the reign of Louis XIV., mendicity had existed to a frightful extent, but it was now confidently anticipated that pauperism would cease. Many oppressive taxes were lightened or altogether removed. Exiles were invited to return. Advances were made at two per cent. to manufacturers and tradesmen of credit. Two millions were devoted to the liberation of prisoners for debt; and large sums unjustly seized by the Chamber of Justice, under the Duc de Noailles, were restored. Hospitals were built and endowed, and an immense boon was conferred upon the public by the establishment of gratuitous instruction at the University of Paris.

These were the immediate fruits of the System; and with such results it is no wonder that its author should become the object of popular idolatry.

Besides those enumerated, many other beneficial measures were contemplated by Law, but unfortunately time was never afforded him for the realisation of his vast designs.

As yet, however, confidence in the System remained unshaken, and the power and popularity of its founder increased. But even at this juncture, when the public infatuation was at its height, when the rise in the shares of the Company was steadily maintained, when the billets de banque were preferred to gold, there were some persons who, seeing further than the mass, and apprehending a crisis at no distant date, began cautiously to convert their paper into gold.

In the first instance, these "Realisers," as they were termed, were almost entirely composed of English, Dutch, and Genoese speculators; but very soon some of the more cautious of the Mississippians followed their example. By a manœuvre concerted among themselves, the price of shares was maintained, by a set of persons who combined together, for a fortnight at twenty thousand livres, and during this time they sold. After inundating the Rue Quincampoix with actions, they carried their notes to the Bank, and converted them into specie.

By publishing edicts calculated to enhance the value of paper, and diminish that of gold, Law endeavoured to defeat these manœuvres, but in spite of all his efforts to counteract them they were still carried on.

"The Banque Royale," says Duhautchamp, in reference to these combinations, "would have always been in a state to pay all the billets presented to it, had not the value of all the paper emanating from the operations of the System been raised by manœuvres to the enormous sum of six millions! People of all conditions, having no other object than to follow the operations of the System, employed the principal dealers to obtain the value of their effects. These merchants, made aware of the manœuvre by the parties who desired to draw them into their operations, sought to profit by the favourable conjuncture which allowed the shareholders sufficient time to get rid of their shares—that is to say, to negotiate their paper imperceptibly, and not by a single stroke. With this design they employed all their funds, not to maintain the shares in a proportionable balance, but to kindle a flame which might last for a few days. The movements of the greedy Mississippians having caused the old shares of the Occident to rise to eighteen and twenty thousand livres, and the new subscriptions in proportion, enabled the principal shareholders, whose porte-feuilles were full of paper, to convert their shares into billets de banque, with as much profit as they could hope to obtain by waiting longer. From this moment they meditated a retreat, and thought seriously of realising their funds, either in specie, jewellery, landed property, personal property, furniture, or anything more solid than paper. The first Realisers having restored gold from the contempt into which it had fallen, the other Mississippians, who perceived the scarceness of the metal, flung themselves upon everything else they could find, and made lands, houses, and goods rise six or seven times above their value."

Further on the same writer remarks: "As to the new men, finding themselves overwhelmed with paper, they made all imaginable efforts to realise; whereby the necessaries of life rose to a most exorbitant price. The drapers and mercers sold at twenty-five crowns the yard cloth for which they had before asked sixteen or eighteen francs—and velvets, silks, and other stuffs in the same proportion. The rents of houses were most exorbitant. In certain pieces of goldsmith's work the graver's labour cost more than double the price of the gold itself. At last all was so upset that sensible persons were perplexed how to act. A prodigious number of new coaches embarrassed the city, so that it was scarcely possible to ap proach the principal streets, especially those leading to the Rue Quincampoix. Three-fourths of the people of the provinces had rushed to Paris: those who could not share in the fortunes already made sought to embark in the new operations. The deputies of companies and corporate bodies who had come up to receive the reimbursement of their rents, had no sooner touched their funds than they carried them off to realise them. Among the great millionnaires, Vernesobre, instead of buying lands and houses, or monopolising merchandise, like Vignolles, another Mississippian, realised thirty millions in gold, and contrived to send it out of the kingdom. Madame Caumont, who had not the same facilities as Vernesobre, who was a cashier at the Bank, pounced upon lands and houses. She bought a quantity of signorial lands, as well in the provinces as in the neighbourhood of Paris, and by this means acquired many superb hotels—amongst others, the Hôtel de Pompone, in the Place des Victoires. The panic which seized those who had not given in to the practices we have described, was doubly disastrous to the credit of the paper by the precipitate sale which they effected when the millionnaires had carried off all the specie and all the billets de banque they could procure; but in spite of all this, the slightest suspicion of a new decree always excited a brisk movement in the Rue Quincampoix—and this served as a pretext to raise or lower the actions. The strongest, who desired to sell largely, boldly announced that the decree would be to the advantage of the paper, and distributed billets de banque; if, on the contrary, they designed to buy a large amount, they interpreted the decree in a different manner, making a manœuvre in the opposite direction. By such management they sustained for more than fifteen days the actions of the Occident at eighteen thousand livres, so as to allow themselves time to make all right."

At this juncture a grand assemblage of the directors and principal shareholders of the Compagnie des Indes took place in the Hôtel Mazarin. The meeting comprised not only the Duc de Bourbon, the Prince de Conti, the Duc de la Force, and many of the aristocracy, but all the new millionnaires, and it was remarked that these parvenus were more splendidly attired than the nobles, and that the equipages awaiting them in the Rue de Richelieu were the finest to be seen there. The Regent presided, but the discussions were conducted by Law.

It appeared, from the statement of the director-general, that the enormous number of six hundred and twenty-four thousand shares had been created, of which the king possessed one hundred thousand, and the company an equal number. The profits of the company were estimated at twelve millions, and Law proposed thenceforward to pay a dividend of forty per cent. on the shares,—an announcement which was received with loud cheers. No one questioned the correctness of Law's statement. He had accomplished so many financial miracles, that to doubt him now was impossible.

Immediately after this meeting, such was the frenzy of the jobbers in the Rue Quincampoix, that the shares mounted higher than ever. But this extraordinary rise chiefly benefited the Realisers, and such heavy drains were made by them upon the Bank, that its vast reserve of gold became perceptibly diminished.

Alarmed at these proceedings, Law endeavoured to check them by an edict which raised the value of the billets de banque five per cent. above that of specie. But, in spite of this, the drain of gold still continued.

As it was absolutely necessary to avert the danger by which the System was threatened, and as this could only be accomplished by getting the whole power into his own hands to baffle the designs of his enemies, Law signified to the Regent that he had at last made up his mind to comply with the conditions which would enable him to accept the office of comptroller-general of finance.

"I am very glad to find you have got rid of your scruples," said the prince, smiling. "Dubois shall send the Abbé Tencin to you to-morrow morning. I have no doubt he will convince you of your errors, and make a good Catholic of you. But what will Lady Catherine say to your conversion? I know she is strongly opposed to it."

"I have not yet communicated my design to her," replied Law. "But whatever arguments she may employ, I shall remain firm."

"I hope so," said the Regent. "As long as this bar to your promotion exists, I cannot help you as I fain would do, neither can I remove your enemy, D'Argenson, from the post of minister of finances. You have done wisely in coming to this decision. Prepare for a visit from the Abbé Tencin to-morrow morning."

II.

HOW LAW BECAME A CONVERT TO THE FAITH OF ROME.

On the following morning, as Law and Lady Catherine were alone together in her ladyship's exquisitely furnished boudoir, which looked upon the magnificent gardens at the back of their hotel, Law, not without some misgiving, opened the matter to her. She heard him with dismay.

"I see that the step I am about to take does not meet your approval," he said; "but let me explain my motives for it. I must either become minister, and so have entire control of the finances of the country, or see the wondrous work I have raised with so much labour perish. I have attained a pinnacle of greatness, but shall be cast down unless I can make my footing secure. You do not comprehend the extraordinary difficulties and dangers that beset a position like mine, or you would not be surprised that I seek to strengthen myself."

Lady Catherine looked at him steadily for a moment, and then said: "If your System can only be saved by the sacrifice of principle you are prepared to make, let it perish, but be true to yourself. Let us retire from this splendour in which we have lived so long, and which has not been altogether productive of happiness. I will readily give it up."

"It cannot be," said Law. "You might as well ask a general to throw down his arms, and quit the field at the moment of victory, as urge me to retreat. What would all France—all Europe—think of my retirement?"

"What will all good men think when they

hear you have abjured your faith?" she rejoined. "But you will not do it."

At this moment Thierry entered, and informed his master that the Abbé Tencin had come according to appointment.

"Show him to my cabinet, and say I will be with him presently," observed Law. And as Thierry departed, he said, with a forced smile, "You can guess the object of the abbé's visit, I suppose?"

"I can," she replied, sadly. "Oh! as you love me—as you would not make me wretched—let me implore you not to go near him! Send him away. Let me use all the influence I possess with you to deter you from the fatal step you are about to take, for fatal I am sure it will be. Nothing but ill consequences will flow from it. Hitherto, prosperity has attended your career, but how can you hope for a continuance of it, if you thus provoke Heaven's anger. You are about to become a proselyte to the faith of Rome, not from conviction, but from unworthy motives—forgive me, if I use strong terms, but you know they are prompted by affection."

"Why should you doubt my sincerity?" rejoined Law. "Why do you assume that I do not really incline to the Romish faith? Let me tell you that I should have joined that Church long ago, but from consideration for you."

"If it be so—though I can scarce believe you," she rejoined, "let consideration for me prevent you from joining that idolatrous Church now."

"Be content, Kate. I do not ask you to become an idolator. You shall have your own way, let me have mine."

"This is the first real unhappiness I have felt since our marriage. Henceforth there will be a bar between us."

"Tut! tut! there will be no bar," he rejoined. "Be reasonable, and dismiss your fears. But mark me, Kate—when the Abbé Tencin has done with me, I wish him to see our children."

"You do not desire that they, too, should be converted?" she cried.

"I have not time for further discussion now," he rejoined, rising from his chair. "Do as I bid you without questioning, Kate."

And he hastily quitted the room.

For a moment Lady Catherine thought of following him, but feeling convinced from his manner that any further attempt to move him would be futile, she sank back in her chair, and gave vent to her affliction in a flood of tears.

She was roused by the entrance of Belinda, who was still a guest at the Hôtel Law.

Lady Catherine told her all that had occurred, adding, "You will acknowledge that I have good reason to be unhappy. This is the heaviest blow that has ever fallen on me."

"You are wrong to take the matter so much to heart," replied Belinda. "For my part, I really cannot blame Mr. Law for the step he is about to take. It is unavoidable. To be comptroller-general he must renounce his religion, and become ostensibly a Catholic. I say *ostensibly*, because I dare say he will secretly be as good a Protestant as ever."

"It may be so—but what dreadful hypocrisy! I shudder to think of it!" exclaimed Lady Catherine.

"Ah! my dear, you must not judge your husband too harshly. He is in a peculiar position."

"And then my children! Why should they be forced to abjure their religion? I will never consent to it—never!" cried Lady Catherine.

"Your son is too young to understand any points of doctrine," said Belinda. "But as regards your daughter, she scarcely requires conversion, for she is more than half a Catholic already. I have my information from a good source—Colombe Laborde."

"If Colombe told you so it must be correct, for she knows Kate's sentiments better than any one else," rejoined Lady Catherine. "I hope

Colombe has not led my poor child into the paths of error."

"Not intentionally, I am certain," said Belinda. "But you must obey your husband's injunctions, Kate."

"I suppose I must," rejoined Lady Catherine. "Oh! Belinda, I begin to be weary of the life I am leading. I am tired of splendour. I am sick of the adulation of these great people, who court me, and pay me homage, only to obtain favours from my husband. I treat them haughtily—not from pride, but because I despise their meanness. I well know their hollowness and insincerity, and that if any reverse were to happen to Mr. Law, they would at once turn their backs upon me."

"Very likely, my dear. 'Tis the way of the world. And this proves how necessary it is for Mr. Law to maintain his position by every means in his power. So don't blame him. For my part, I think him the best and kindest of men, and I am sure he is always actuated by high and honourable motives."

"You do him no more than justice, Belinda. But I wish he would remain true to his religion."

"Well, as it can't be helped, you must submit. But let us change the subject, and return to Colombe. I wish we could see her united to Evelyn Harcourt. Is there any chance of it?"

"I begin to despair," replied Lady Catherine. "M. Laborde is still obdurate as ever, and insists upon the fulfilment of her engagement with M. Cossard. The utmost I have been able to accomplish has been to delay the marriage from time to time on one pretext or another, in the hope that Cossard's patience would be exhausted, and that he would retire in disgust, but I have been disappointed."

"Poor Colombe! I pity her much. She is a charming girl, and deserves a better fate than to be sacrificed to such an odious wretch as Cossard.

No one knows better than myself how unhappy a woman is who is tied to a man she cannot love, and were Colombe wedded to this Cossard she would be miserable, as I was in my first marriage. You will have other anxieties soon, Kate. In a year or two you will have to choose a husband for your daughter."

"We have already plenty of suitors," replied Lady Catherine. "Yesterday we had an offer from the Prince de Tarento; and I may say, without boasting, that her hand has been sought by representatives of the noblest families of France, Germany, Italy, and England. But the husband I have in view for her is her cousin, Lord Wallingford."

"And a very good husband he would make her, no doubt," replied Belinda. "But don't force her inclinations."

"That I will never do," said Lady Catherine. "Neither will Mr. Law; and for this reason he will not entertain any proposition, however important, at present. But I must now go and prepare my children for an interview with the Abbé Tencin," said Lady Catherine. "My heart revolts from the task."

"Let me go with you," said Belinda. "I may be of use."

And they quitted the room together.

As may be imagined, the Abbé Tencin did not experience much difficulty in the work of conversion, and after a few visits he declared that his illustrious proselyte was in a fit state to be received into the bosom of the Church of Rome.

The abjuration of heresy was solemnised with great pomp in the church of Saint Roch, in the presence of a vast assemblage, which comprehended all the highest nobility; and Law, with his son and daughter, who attended with him, having made public profession of the Romish faith, were admitted into the communion of that Church.

For this labour in the cause of his religion the Abbé Tencin received a gratification of two hundred thousand livres, and as the sacred edifice in which the ceremonial took place was at that time in an unfinished state, Law, with his usual liberality, bestowed five hundred thousand livres for its completion.

III.

OF THE QUARREL BETWEEN LAW AND THE EARL OF STAIR.

LAW'S conversion by the Abbé Tencin, who afterwards became a cardinal, gave rise to the following pasquil:

> Fi de ton zèle séraphique,
> Malheureux Abbé de Tencin;
> Depuis que Law est Catholique,
> Tout le royaume est capucin.

The event was celebrated by a grand entertainment given by the Duc de Bourbon, at which the Regent and the whole of the court were present.

Among the many distinguished guests assembled

on this occasion was the British ambassador, the Earl of Stair; and in the course of the evening his lordship found an opportunity of saying a few words in private to the Regent.

"Monseigneur," he began, "I am sure you would regret that anything should occur to disturb the good understanding at present subsisting between the court of my royal master and that of your highness."

"Your excellency is quite right," rejoined the Regent. "I should greatly regret it. But I see no chance of our friendly relations being interrupted. To what do you allude?"

"I will speak frankly," replied Lord Stair. "It is generally understood that Mr. Law's conversion, which has taken place this day, and which we are here met to celebrate, is a preliminary step to his elevation to the office of comptroller-general of finance."

"Suppose it to be so, what then?" rejoined the Regent, coldly.

"I have only to remark, monseigneur, that the appointment could not be agreeable to my royal master, because Mr. Law's predilections are known to be favourable to the fallen dynasty. Indeed, I have proof that letters have passed between him and the Chevalier de Saint George."

"Your excellency's information is correct," said the Regent, "but as you may possibly be ignorant of the purport of those letters, I will acquaint you with it. At your instance, my lord, the pension allowed to the proscribed royal family by his late majesty, Louis XIV., was discontinued; but since M. Law has risen to his present eminence, and has become the dispenser of so many bounties, the unfortunate prince wrote to him thus—I will give the precise words: 'I address myself to you as to a good Scotsman, and a faithful servant of the Regent, and I ask you to assist me.' The letter was laid before me by M. Law, who besought my permission to pay out of his own funds the pension which had been stopped at the

Treasury. Of course I could not refuse the request."

"Mr. Law may have been influenced by worthy motives in this affair," said the ambassador; "but I think his generosity ill judged. It is certain to be misconstrued. The circumstance mentioned by your highness strengthens my opinion that the appointment will be unsatisfactory to my royal master. Mr. Law must be regarded as an enemy of England. He has been heard to boast that he will ruin our trade and commerce, and make us subsidiary to France."

"I never heard him make such a boast," replied the Regent. "But your lordship cannot complain of fair rivalry. You cannot expect us to forego advantages to please you."

"I am not foolish enough to expect such concession, monseigneur," rejoined Lord Stair. "But I am too well aware of Mr. Law's disposition towards the country of his birth not to feel uneasy at his accession to power. I am certain it will be his aim to cause a disagreement between your highness and the king my master. Only a few days ago he announced to some friends of mine his intention of publishing a treatise, to prove that it is impossible for Great Britain to pay her debts."

"If your country is solvent, the book will do no harm," laughed the Regent.

"The book may not, monseigneur, but its author may. As comptroller-general, Mr. Law will be in a condition to damage my country, and everything indicates that he will try to do so. We stand too much in the way of his ambitious designs to allow him to look upon us with a friendly eye. All these things considered, I repeat, that the elevation of such a man to the chief post of your government must be displeasing to the king my master, and I would fain hope the appointment may not take place."

"Your excellency is uneasy without cause," said the Regent. "M. Law is resolved to advance the prosperity of France to the highest possible point, but not at the expense of Great Britain. As to the rest, I will take good care there shall be no misunderstanding between the two courts."

"Your highness is then resolved to make this adventurer prime minister?" said Lord Stair, unable to control himself.

"If I had not previously intended to do so, your excellency's observations would decide me," replied the Regent, with dignity. "I shall appoint a minister, not to please England, but to serve France."

At this moment Law himself appeared, and seeing them engaged in discourse, was about to retire, when the Regent called him back, saying, "We have been talking about you."

"I have no wish to disguise my opinions," said Lord Stair. "I hope your highness will tell Mr. Law that I object to his appointment to the office of comptroller-general for two reasons. First, that he is a secret friend of the Pretender; secondly, that he is the avowed enemy of Great Britain."

"If I am the avowed enemy of England, my lord—though I deny that I am so—you need fear no perfidy on my part," rejoined Law. "Had the unfortunate James Stuart perished at Nonancourt by the hand of the assassin Douglas, my assistance would not have been required. But as the prince happily escaped that foul plot, I have aided him, and shall continue to aid him as long as I am permitted to do so by his Highness the Regent."

At this allusion to the dark design of which he was known to be the instigator, Lord Stair became livid with rage.

"And now, monseigneur," pursued Law, turning to the Regent, "I have a word to say to Lord Stair on my own account. I charge him with being the author of a plot against me—not to take away my life, as he would have done that of the Chevalier de Saint George, but to destroy my credit. The late attack upon the Bank was his contrivance. Of this I have ample proof."

"It is a calumny," rejoined the ambassador. "I may have said to certain of my countrymen that I prefer specie to your paper, and they may have acted on the hint, and repaired to the Bank, but as to any combination, I repudiate the charge, and challenge you to make good the assertion. I trust your highness will hesitate before committing the guidance of the state-chariot to this modern Phaeton. Most assuredly he will upset it."

"You go too far in your remarks, my lord," said the Regent. "M. Law is now virtually comptroller-general. Let me hope that this difference between you may be adjusted."

"Impossible, monseigneur," said Law. "After what has passed between Lord Stair and myself, not even official intercourse can take place between us."

"Then, my lord," said the Regent, turning to

the ambassador, "I shall be compelled to ask your recal."

"I am sorry to have lost the personal credit I have so long enjoyed with your highness," replied Lord Stair, "but I have spoken with candour, and you will one day, I feel convinced, admit that I have given you good counsel."

And with a profound obeisance to the Regent, and a haughty bow to Law, he withdrew.

All difficulties being removed, the Regent conferred upon Law the title of Comptroller-General of Finance, and D'Argenson had the bitter mortification of surrendering his post to the rival he detested, and was obliged to content himself with the office of keeper of the seals.

Law had now reached the pinnacle of his ambition. He had become the equal of the highest nobility of the kingdom—nay, their superior. He had triumphed over all his enemies, and as the Regent was entirely guided by his counsels, he might be said to hold the reins of government in his own hands. In the space of four years, to employ the language of Voltaire, he had literally become, from a Scotsman, a Frenchman by naturalisation; from a Protestant, a Catholic; from an adventurer, the lord of the finest estates in the kingdom; and from a banker, prime minister.

The power and ability of the new comptroller-general were not merely recognised by the nation thus placed under his governance, but by all the great states of Europe, and the British ministry, finding that Lord Stair had irritated him, and was personally disagreeable to him, determined to recal that ambassador, and with this design immediately despatched Earl Stanhope, one of the secretaries of state, to Paris.

The popular enthusiasm, which found expression in a hundred different ways, satisfied the Regent that his choice of a minister was eminently agreeable to the nation at large. All ranks of society vied with each other in paying court to the new comptroller-general. Honours were showered upon him more thickly than ever, and his portrait was everywhere to be seen, with these lines affixed to it:

> Principe sub recto Gallorum sceptra tenente,
> Publica nunc rectè Quæstor hic aera regit:
> Aeraque tractandi summâ perfectus in arte,
> Et regem et populum divitem utrumque fecit.

Honours from abroad were paid him, and the freedom of his native city of Edinburgh was transmitted to him in a valuable gold box.

It was at this time that Law negotiated with Lord Londonderry for the purchase of the famous Pitt diamond, which afterwards became the brightest ornament of the French crown. This diamond, which was nearly as large as a pigeon's egg, of exquisite purity, and astonishing brilliancy, received the name of "The Regent."

To prove his admiration of Law's genius, the Earl of Islay republished one of the great financier's early treatises, to which he affixed this motto from Cicero, "O terram illam beatam qui hunc virum exceperit; hanc ingratam si ejecerit, miseram si amiserit."

The splendour of Law's mode of life increased with the elevation he had attained. He still continued to occupy the same hotel as heretofore in the Place Vendôme, but his large establishment was considerably augmented, and his banquets and fêtes were more sumptuous than ever. But no distractions of pleasure were ever allowed to interfere with his attention to affairs of state, all his available time and energies being unremittingly devoted to the fulfilment of his duties.

It was at this moment, when he was apparently most secure, when all were paying him homage, when the streets resounded with his name, and when acclamations attended his appearance, that intimations of the terrible defeat he was about to experience began to be felt.

IV.

HOW SPECIE WAS PROSCRIBED BY LAW.

THE constant drain of specie from the Bank still continuing, Law was forced to adopt measures from which he had hitherto abstained. Determined to push the System to its utmost limits, he now prohibited the payment in gold of any sum exceeding three hundred livres. Bills of exchange were to be paid only in bank-notes, and creditors were empowered to demand notes from their debtors.

After resorting to every expedient to give to paper the preference to gold and silver, the comptroller-general issued a decree entirely abolishing the use of specie, except certain pieces of little value which had been recently coined. By this decree it was ordained that no person, of whatever condition, not even a member of a religious community, should keep more than five hundred livres in specie, on pain of confiscation of all exceeding that amount, with a fine of ten thousand livres. Another decree prohibited, under a penalty of three thousand livres, the payment of a sum of a hundred livres or upwards except in billets de banque.

To enforce strict fulfilment of these edicts, domiciliary visits were authorised, and all the rigours practised by the Chamber of Justice, under the Duc de Noailles, were revived. As at that frightful period, informers were encouraged and rewarded with half the treasure seized. No habitations were exempted from search. The hotels of the nobles, privileged places, religious houses, palaces and royal mansions, were visited.

But these severe enactments were violated with

impunity by certain exalted personages. In defiance of the edict, the Prince de Conti paid all the notes in his possession into the Bank, and Law, unwilling to offend him, allowed him to carry off gold and silver sufficient to fill three waggons.

The offender was sharply reprimanded for his conduct by the Regent, but this did not deter the Duc de Bourbon from following his brother's example, and he obtained specie to the amount of twenty-five millions.

Justly indignant at this proceeding, the Regent sent for the duke, and addressed him thus:

"I am very angry with you, M. le Duc. It seems to me that you wish to destroy in a single moment the fabric which it has cost M. Law so much time and pains to erect. You empty the Bank by drawing from it twenty-five millions in four days—while the Prince de Conti has taken out twenty-five millions at the same time. What will you both do with so much money? Are you and your brother acting in conformity with the last ordinance of his majesty, which prohibits all his subjects, without exception, from having more than five hundred livres in specie in their possession? Answer me that question, M. le Duc."

"I admit that I have cashed twenty-five millions at the Bank, monseigneur," replied the duke, in a deprecatory tone. "But the money is all gone."

"All gone! Impossible!" cried the Regent.

"It is nevertheless true, monseigneur. It has been swept away as if by magic. Let the commissioners pay me a visit. They will find nothing."

"Bah! you have taken good care to hide the money."

"It is hidden in the pockets of my creditors, monseigneur. I have not touched a single louis d'or."

"It would serve you right to compel you to

render a strict account of the gold you have taken, M. le Duc; and were it not for the scandal which such a course must occasion, I would do so. It is unworthy of you and the Prince de Conti to act thus. Think of the injurious effect your proceedings will have upon the Bank."

"Our proceedings will benefit the Bank, monseigneur, by proving that it has an ample reserve fund of gold."

"Well, have you done all the mischief you intend? Have you any more billets de banque left?"

"Only a million or two, which I require for my own private expenditure," replied the duke. "I promise not to disturb the Bank again. I am sorry to find M. Law has been so much embarrassed by the Realisers."

"The Realisers who have most embarrassed him, M. le Duc, are yourself and the Prince de Conti."

"Well, I will let him alone in future—nay,

more, I will support him in all his measures against the Realisers. Gold, I am informed, has been sent away in prodigious quantities into England."

"I hope the drain is now stopped," said the Regent. "A vast deal of specie has been recently paid in. The former chancellor, M. de Pontchartrain, has sent in fifty-seven thousand louis d'or of the old coinage, each worth sixty-two francs, and many others have paid in large sums. Besides this, several important seizures have been recently made by the commissioners. Six thousand gold marcs and twenty thousand silver marcs were found in the house of a paper-maker named Sohier. Fifty thousand marcs in gold and silver were likewise discovered in the house of M. Dupin. Forty millions in gold have been seized on the frontiers of Switzerland. But the capture most gratifying to the comptroller-general has been fourteen millions which the Frères Paris had secretly transmitted into Lorraine, in order to purchase lands."

"I am glad Frères Paris have been caught,"

said the duke. "And I rejoice to think that the coffers of the Bank have been so abundantly replenished. I hope that, like the cask of the Danaides, they may not be emptied as soon as filled."

"We will take care to prevent that," said the Regent.

"The immense deposits alluded to by your highness," observed the duke, "will revive the spirits of the Mississippians, and cause them to speculate again as briskly as ever. Is there to be a fresh issue of shares?"

"Not at present," replied the Regent. "The shares already issued amount to more than six milliards."

"Another milliard will not signify," observed the duke, laughing.

"Another milliard would destroy the System," said the Regent.

"Not if paper can be substituted for specie," observed the duke. "Since gold and silver are proscribed, we shall now be able to test the correctness of M. Law's scheme."

"I am confident it will stand the test applied to it," said the Regent.

"Hum! we shall see," rejoined the duke. "At all events, I am on the safe side," he mentally ejaculated.

At this moment, the President Lambert de Vernon was announced by the usher, and the Duc de Bourbon took his departure, secretly congratulating himself on having escaped so well.

"To what am I indebted for this visit, M. le Président?" inquired the Regent of Vernon, as soon as they were alone.

"Monseigneur," replied the other, "I am come to denounce a certain individual who has in his possession five hundred thousand livres in gold."

"What! M. le Président?" cried the Regent, contemptuously. "Is it on such an infamous errand that you have come to me? Would you turn informer?"

"Monseigneur, I simply fulfil your own ordinance. You have made the law, and I must perforce obey it."

"Very true," replied the Regent, sternly. "And I suppose you expect the informer's fee?"

"Naturally, monseigneur. I expect two hundred and fifty thousand livres."

"You shall have them, if you choose to disgrace yourself by accepting them."

"It will be no disgrace to me, monseigneur. On the contrary, I shall save half my fortune. The person I have come to denounce is myself."

"Aha! a clever ruse!" cried the Regent, laughing. "Well, you shall keep half your gold."

"I humbly thank your highness. I would rather have it than ten times the amount in paper."

"Fi, M. le Président. Don't say a word against the billets de banque, or I shall compel you to pay in the whole amount."

V.

THE BANDOLIERS OF THE MISSISSIPPI.

A GREAT deal of popular discontent was caused at this time by the arbitrary proceedings adopted by the comptroller-general for the colonisation of the Mississippi. The vagabonds and fugitives from justice, who had been transported in the first instance to the new colony, having caused much disorder, recruits were now sought among those whose sole crime was poverty. All the houses of refuge for the poor were emptied, the Hospital, Bicêtre, La Pitié, La Salpêtrière, Les Enfants-Trouvés, each furnishing their quota. Discharged servants, and workmen out of employ, were likewise seized. These forcible abductions caused great uneasiness, especially among the poorer classes, who naturally felt that their own turn might come.

Two companies of archers were formed, whose business it was to arrest all persons unable to give a satisfactory account of themselves. From their costume and equipments, these archers were denominated "Bandoliers of the Mississippi." They wore long blue coats, broad cross-belts, and hats laced with silver, and were armed with swords, muskets, and pistols. Marching about in detachments of a dozen, with an officer at their head, the bandoliers performed their task with so much zeal, that five thousand persons were carried off by them in ten days. Many of these were artisans and workmen, but a large proportion consisted of young women. These unjust arrests, and the shocking treatment to which the captives were subjected, roused the popular indignation.

At last an incident occurred which well-nigh

caused a general rising. A hundred country maidens, who had come to Paris in quest of service, and had found a temporary asylum with the good Sisters of Saint Catherine's Hospital, suddenly disappeared. It was supposed they had been carried off by the bandoliers of the Mississippi. While this question was being discussed by an incensed mob, the bandoliers were seen carrying off two young persons. Exasperated beyond endurance by this spectacle, the populace armed themselves with such implements as came readiest to hand, and set upon the archers. Twenty were killed upon the spot, and a still greater number were carried in a dying state to the Hôtel-Dieu. This conflict produced but little effect. A proclamation was made by sound of trump that each brigade of bandoliers should be accompanied by an exempt of police, and the bandoliers were expressly forbidden, under heavy penalties, from arresting any citizen, artisan, or journeyman labourer, or any other person, not a pauper; but, in spite of this, the arrests were soon conducted with as much recklessness and inhumanity as before, to the great prejudice of the comptroller-general's popularity.

VI.

IN WHICH COSSARD MAKES A CONFIDENTIAL COMMUNICATION TO LABORDE.

WHILE the arbitrary measures we have described were being taken by Law to support the System, the directors of the Compagnie des Indes were not without strong apprehensions of an approaching crisis.

One day Cossard invited Laborde to a tête-à-tête dinner at his charming maison de plaisance, and after the repast, when all the attendants had retired, he said,

"I want to have some confidential talk to you,

my good friend, about the position of the Company. I do not desire to alarm you, but it would be improper to conceal from you that its affairs are in a very critical state, and I do not think M. Law will be able to avert the dangers by which he is menaced."

"I have felt this for some time," said Laborde; "and I need not say our position gives me the greatest uneasiness. A depreciation in the value of our stock has already taken place, and unless the downward tendency can be checked, the credit of the Company must go, and we shall be crushed by the fall of the edifice."

"That is quite certain, unless we take timely precautions for our safety," said Cossard.

"But it is now too late," groaned Laborde. "All our gold is gone. On the publication of the edict I paid twenty thousand louis d'or into the Bank."

"Not a single coin of which will you get back," remarked Cossard.

"I fear not. But I suffered too much at the time of the Visa to run the risk of being denounced again."

"Some risk must be run," said Cossard. "We may as well be ruined now as when the general crash comes—as come it certainly will, and that before long. What a pity you did not realise sooner!"

"You blame me, but I fear you have not acted more prudently yourself."

"You are mistaken," said Cossard, with a cunning look, and bringing his chair close to him as he spoke. "I have not been so imprudent as you suppose. I *have* secretly realised. I have got forty millions of livres out of the fire, and, what is more, I have them safe."

"Forty millions!" exclaimed Laborde. "I rejoice to hear it. I won't ask what you have done with the money, but you say you have secured it."

"It is out of the reach of the commissaries,"

replied Cossard. "I have no secrets from you. I have contrived to remit the whole amount to London, whither I shall shortly follow it."

"But how will you accomplish this?" cried Laborde. "I will own to you that I once thought of flying into Holland myself. But the risk is too great. No one is allowed to leave the country. How will you obtain a passport?"

"I have already got one," said Cossard. "All my preparations for flight are made."

"Then you don't intend to fulfil your engagement to Colombe?" said Laborde.

"Pardon me," rejoined Cossard, "that is the very point I am approaching. I hope to take Colombe with me, and, as you will see, it is of the utmost importance that the marriage should take place without delay. Once married to your daughter, I will carry her to my château in Normandy, and thence pass over into England. You must find means to join us in London."

After considerable hesitation and misgiving,

Laborde agreed to the plan, and next morning proceeded to the Hôtel Law, where he had a private interview with his daughter, and explained to her that for many reasons the marriage she had contracted with Cossard could no longer be delayed. Finding he produced but little impression, he said:

"I will give you three days for reflection. If, at the end of that time, you are prepared to obey me and marry Cossard, well and good. If not, you are no longer daughter of mine. You now know my fixed determination."

With this he took his departure, leaving Colombe drowned in tears. He next went to Cossard, and told him what he had done. His intended son-in-law did not appear entirely satisfied with the arrangement, but said,

"I must have a positive answer from Colombe at the time you have appointed. I will submit to no further delay."

"I don't expect it," replied Laborde. "You

have been too much trifled with already. I have laid my paternal injunctions on Colombe, and she will not dare to disobey me. Come to the Hôtel Law on the morning I have fixed for her decision, and I engage to deliver her to you."

On the following day Laborde heard a rumour that greatly alarmed him. It was to the effect that a director, whose name was kept secret, had been 'realizing' largely, and the matter was then under investigation. On hearing this he went immediately to his intended son-in-law, to put him upon his guard, but Cossard manifested no uneasiness.

"Let them pursue their investigations," he said. "I am not afraid. There are reports of this kind every day. Nothing can be proved against me. I am going into the country, but I shall return to-morrow evening, and will meet you at the Hôtel Law at the appointed hour on the following morning."

During this interval Laborde had seen nothing

of his daughter, deeming it best not to go near her, but he was fully determined to carry his point. Accordingly, at the hour agreed upon he made his appearance, and found Colombe with Lady Catherine Law.

"At Colombe's request I have consented to be present at this interview," said her ladyship. "In fact, she wishes me to communicate her decision to you. Will you permit me to state it?"

"No, miladi. I must have my daughter's decision from her own lips. Are you prepared to obey me, Colombe?"

"I cannot," she replied, distractedly. "Indeed, I cannot. Oh, dear Lady Catherine, plead for me! —plead for me! My only hope is in you."

"It is cruel of you to treat your daughter thus, M. Laborde," said Lady Catherine. "She would obey you if she could!"

Laborde, however, was too much excited to attend to her, but addressed himself to Colombe.

"I know why you thus thwart me," he cried.

"But hope not to wed Evelyn Harcourt. Never will I consent to your union with him—never! I swear it!"

At this moment Law entered the room. Laborde was about to take his departure, but Law stopped him.

"If I mistake not you are come here to arrange about Colombe's marriage with Cossard?" he said.

"I came for that purpose, monseigneur," replied Laborde.

"Then attend to me," said Law. "The marriage cannot take place. Cossard has disappeared. We have ascertained that he obtained forty millions in gold from the Bank, and has remitted the amount to London. In all probability he is on his way thither, but the commissionnaires are on his track, and I do not think he will escape them."

"And this is the wretch to whom you would have sacrificed your daughter?" cried Lady Catherine. "But it is not too late to make her amends for all the anguish you have caused her.

Give her to the man of her heart—to Evelyn Harcourt."

"I cannot," replied Laborde, in broken accents. "I have just sworn that I never will consent to her marriage with him."

And he hurried out of the room.

End of the Sixth Book.

BOOK VII.

THE COMTE DE HORN.

I.

HOW THE COMTE DE HORN AND HIS FRIENDS BECAME EMBARRASSED; AND IN WHAT WAY THEIR FUNDS WERE RECRUITED.

NOTWITHSTANDING the symptoms of an approaching crisis, the fury for stock-jobbing continued as great as ever, and the crowds in the Rue Quincampoix were undiminished. So long as paper would serve their turn, and procure them all the material enjoyments they desired, the Mississippians cared not for specie, but, on the contrary, affected to despise it. Having an apparently inexhaustible supply of wealth, they heeded not what they paid.

Luxuries they would have, be the cost what it might. Their prodigalities were unbounded, and never, perhaps, except during the decadence of Rome, was so much license indulged in as by the Mississippians at this period.

Amongst the most dissolute and extravagant of the many profligates then to be found in Paris, were the Comte de Horn and his two inseparable companions De Mille and D'Etampes. Their days were passed in the Rue Quincampoix, and their nights in the gambling-houses and taverns. Their revels and excesses were the wonder of all who heard of them.

For a time they were fortunate in their speculations, and able to carry on their reckless career; but their prodigalities and losses at play emptied their porte-feuilles, and they began to grow embarrassed. Whenever he was in want of funds, De Mille applied without hesitation to Cossard, and never failed to obtain what he wanted. The disappearance of the director was, therefore, a very heavy blow to him, as it cut off a source of supply on which he had hitherto counted. To make matters worse, Cossard's flight occurred at a time when the trio were sadly in want of money.

"What a rascal the fellow must be to decamp in this manner, without giving us the slightest notice of his intentions," cried De Horn. "He has used us infamously."

"They say he has remitted forty millions in gold to London," said De Mille. "If I had suspected his design he should not have got off without leaving two or three millions behind him. I am vexed at my own stupidity. I ought to have known he was a rogue."

"We must pay him a visit in London by-and-by, and see what can be made of him," said D'Etampes. "Meantime, our purses are empty."

"We must look to you, De Mille, to recruit our funds," said De Horn.

"I will try what I can do," replied the individual appealed to; "but I am by no means sanguine of success."

Shortly after this he set out with the intention of applying to his father. Ascertaining at the Bank that M. Laborde was gone to the Hôtel Law, he proceeded thither, and telling the Swiss porters that he had business of the utmost importance with M. Laborde, he was allowed admittance, and was ushered by Thierry into a salon, in which he found his father and sister. As soon as he had recovered from the astonishment into which he was thrown by this unlooked-for and most unwelcome visit, Laborde demanded of his son, in a stern voice, how he dared thus to intrude himself; adding, that if he did not retire instantly, he would cause him to be ejected by the servants.

"For your own sake I advise you not to adopt such a course," rejoined De Mille. "Have you not a word to say to me, Colombe?" he added, turning to her. "It is long since I have seen you. If you have forgotten that you have a brother, I have not forgotten that I have a sister, to whom I am as fondly attached as ever."

"Colombe is not to be imposed upon by this idle profession of regard," interposed Laborde, sternly.

"By Heaven, I speak the truth!" cried De Mille. "Colombe is the sole being whom I really love. Speak to me, sister. I would rather have your reproaches than you should remain silent."

"I do not desire to reproach you, Raoul," she said. "But you have caused me so much grief—so much shame—that I cannot behold you without pain. The sight of you opens wounds which I thought were for ever closed. If you had changed your mode of life, I should be glad to see you again, but I know you are as reckless and profligate as ever."

"I see how it is," rejoined De Mille. "Cossard has calumniated me. Talking of Cossard, let me congratulate you on your liberation from that odious person. You will now be able to marry Evelyn Harcourt."

"No more of this," interposed his father. "An end must be put to an interview which is painful both to me and to Colombe. It is idle to ask why you have come here, when I know you can have but one object—money."

"It would be improper to contradict you, sir," replied De Mille. "I am dreadfully in want of money."

"I knew it," cried his father. "And why should I supply you with funds to continue your disorders and debauchery?—no! no! you shall have no money from me."

"I must have three or four thousand livres," rejoined De Mille. "I don't intend to go hence without it," he added, seating himself, coolly.

"Villain! robber! you will drive me to do something desperate!" cried his father, shaking his clenched hand in his face, but only provoking a smile from De Mille.

"You had better accede to his demands, dear father, and let him go!" said Colombe.

"I am in no hurry," observed De Mille. "I am very comfortable here, and will wait till the old gentleman is perfectly cool."

"I shall go mad!" cried Laborde, trembling with passion.

"Better give me the money than do that," laughed De Mille.

"Let him have it—let him have it, dear father!" said Colombe. "Lady Catherine Law or Kate may come in, and then an explanation must ensue."

Perceiving he had gained his point, De Mille became quite easy. After a desperate struggle with himself, Laborde took out a porte-feuille, and said:

"Well, you shall have the money. But it is the last you will ever get from me."

"That remains to be seen," muttered his son. "I felt sure you would think better of it, sir," he added, aloud.

"This porte-feuille contains six thousand livres," said his father, giving it him—"double the amount you have asked for. Make good use of it, if you can."

"I will make the best possible use of it, sir, by taking it to the Fair of Saint-Germain to-morrow," replied De Mille. "I trust I shall not have to apply to you again."

"You may spare yourself the trouble. You shan't have another livre from me—not if it would save you from the executioner."

"Stay a moment, Raoul," said Colombe. "This money will enable you to quit Paris. Fly from temptations which will lead you to destruction."

"I have no intention of leaving Paris. I find it far too agreeable," replied De Mille.

And, bowing to his father, who turned from him in disgust, he quitted the room.

II.

THE FAIR OF SAINT-GERMAIN.

NEVER before had the Fair of Saint-Germain been so well attended as during the year in which the System was in vogue. Booths, theatres, gaming-houses, cabarets, cafés, wine-shops, and all other places of amusement were thronged.

The Fair, which was kept open for several weeks, was held in a large meadow contiguous to the ancient Abbey of Saint-Germain-des-Prés, to which wealthy religious establishment the revenues arising from the annual meeting accrued.

The ground was divided into regular streets, consisting of booths or shops, built with timber; the principal streets on the side of the Rue des Quatre-Vents, by which the Fair was approached from the north, being occupied by dealers in bijouterie, ivory, sculpture, pictures, and wearing apparel. Here also were several cafés and cabarets. In other streets were booths in which were to be seen jugglers, rope-dancers, mountebanks, and marionnettes. Besides these, there were caravans containing wild beasts, then a novelty to the Parisians. In the Fair there were no less than four large theatres, at which the principal actors from the regular theatres performed, and there was also a large building, in which masked balls and ballets were given.

The mania for gambling then prevailing in Paris was strongly displayed at the Fair of Saint-Germain, and at the cafés, cabarets, and tripots, with which the place abounded, stock-jobbing was conducted as in the Rue Quincampoix. Speculation, in fact, had become a necessity of existence to the Mississippians.

Although a police-regulation in force at the time interdicted play, under a penalty of three thousand livres, there were several gambling-houses where cards, dice, biribi, faro, lansquenet, and other games of chance were openly played. In these tripots, billets de banque for fifty or sixty thousand livres were staked on a card or a cast of the die by the Mississippians, with as much unconcern as if the notes had been mere waste paper. Play, however, was not confined to the gambling-houses and cabarets, but went on in all the shops, where the tradesmen provided cards and dice for their customers, while the bystanders betted on the play.

The Fair of Saint-Germain, which, as we have shown, was the grand rendezvous of all the dissipated society of Paris—and at no period was society so dissipated as during the Regency—had special attractions for the Comte de Horn and his profligate companions, and it will not appear surprising that, after the opening of the Fair, they should abandon the Rue Quincampoix for the new scene of dissipation, and spend the whole of their time in mingling with the amusements of the place, doing business with the stock-jobbers in the cafés, playing at biribi or hazard with the dealers in bijouterie, gambling desperately in the tripots, revelling in the cabarets, and creating disturbances at the theatres and in the salle de danse.

During all this time a constant run of ill luck attended the Comte de Horn. He was unlucky in his speculations, and still more unlucky at play, and had it not been that his companions were somewhat more fortunate, and shared their purses with him, he would have been in a desperate plight. It was while haunting the Fair of Saint-Germain, and living in the dissolute manner we have described, that De Mille became acquainted with a number of reckless spendthrifts, whose habits and principles were congenial to his own, and he began to organise a body of desperadoes calculated to aid him in carrying out a scheme which he had conceived of wholesale plunder in the Rue Quincampoix.

The Comte de Horn, as we have already mentioned, was connected with the noblest families in the Low Countries, and one day, meeting his cousin, the young Duc d'Aremberg, a prince of the Pays Bas, he invited him to sup with him at the Vieux Loup, the principal tavern in the Fair of Saint-Germain, where good cheer and excellent wine could be obtained, though at a most extravagant rate. The whole night was spent in revelry, the young topers trying who could drink most. Incredible was the number of flasks they emptied. About six o'clock in the morning they sallied forth, ready for any mischief, and followed by their lacqueys, each of whom bore a bottle of champagne and a goblet. After wandering through the deserted streets of the Fair, and disturbing the occupants of the booths by their shouts, they resolved to seek amusement elsewhere, and, passing along the Rue de Varennes and the Rue du Four, made their way into the Pont-Neuf, where they stopped to salute the equestrian statue of Henri Quatre, and drank a glass to the memory of the "vert galant" monarch, after which they proceeded towards the church of Saint-Germain-l'Auxerrois.

As they entered the open space in front of this noble pile, one of the finest specimens of ecclesiastical architecture in Paris, they encountered a dismal procession, which ought to have put serious thoughts into their heads.

A bier, sustaining a coffin covered with a pall, surrounded by lighted tapers and candles, and provided with an aspersorium, was being borne slowly towards the porch of the church.

"Who goes there?" demanded the Comte de Horn of an old man who was kneeling on the ground in the path of the procession. "Who is being taken to his last home, I say, coquin?" he repeated.

"'Tis the Sieur Nigon, the procureur," replied the man. "He used to live in yonder cloister."

"What! my old friend, Nigon!" cried De Horn, who had never heard of the defunct procureur before. "So he is gone. Poor fellow! I must bid him adieu."

So saying, he staggered forward, and placing himself in the way of the bier, ordered the bearers to halt and set down their load.

"Do not interrupt us in the performance of our duty," said a priest, advancing. He was a venerable-looking man, with a mild expression of countenance. "Stand aside and let us pass."

But, instead of complying, De Horn and his companions, attended by the lacqueys, surrounded the bier, and the count plucking aside the pall, disclosed the ghastly features of the dead man—the coffin being unclosed.

"Ah! my poor dear Nigon!" he cried. "I recognise you now. And so you have been foolish enough to die, eh? What was the cause of your death, my poor friend? Thirst, no doubt. Thirst kills us all. I should die if I didn't drink. To drink is to live. Wine will revive you. Drink, I say, my friend." And taking a goblet of champagne from his servant, he held it towards the corpse, continuing thus: "Cast off that hideous black mantle, quit these crows, and come and make merry with us."

"Cease this irreverent talk, and depart," cried the priest, "or I shall call upon those around me to drive you hence."

By this time a crowd had collected near the spot, but they were kept off by De Mille and the others who had drawn their swords.

"I tell you my worthy friend, Nigon, died of thirst," cried De Horn. "He must have something to drink. If you won't allow him wine, he shall have water."

With this he vaulted upon the bier, and bestriding the coffin, seized the bénitier, and poured its contents upon the face of the deceased, calling out, "Drink, my poor friend, drink!"

"This is an act of dreadful impiety," cried the

priest, horror-stricken. "Thou art a wretch abandoned of heaven, and the curse of the Church will fall upon thee and upon thy godless companions."

Scandalised by the impious proceeding, the crowd made a rush upon the young men, and succeeded in disarming them, while the priest's attendants dragged De Horn from the bier. In the scuffle, however, the tapers were extinguished, and the pall was much damaged.

Anxious to prevent further disturbance, and having far more consideration for the profane young men than they deserved, the good priest ordered the bearers to convey the bier quickly into the church, and they accomplished their task without further interruption.

Scarcely, however, had the bier passed through the door of the sacred edifice, than a hawker appeared on the place, calling out the last ordinance relating to a new coinage of silver crowns, which were termed in derision "les enfants morts nés."

On hearing this, De Horn and the others went up to the hawker, and each procuring a copy of the arrêt, they marched towards the church, followed by the crowd, who were curious to see what would ensue. Luckily for himself at this juncture, the Duc d'Aremberg fell down in a state of drunken insensibility, and was carried off by the lacqueys.

On entering the church, De Horn and the two others remained standing quietly in one of the aisles, until the priests and choristers commenced the requiem, when they came forward and chanted in a loud voice the title and terms of the decree. Such irreverence was not to be endured. The service was instantly stopped, and an end was put to the scandal by the appearance of the archers of the grande-prévôté, by whom the offenders were taken into custody, and brought before M. de Machault, the lieutenant-general of police. By him they were sent to the Bastille.

When particulars of the occurrence were related to the Regent, he laughed heartily, but Law, who was with him at the time, shook his head, and said it was a sinister event, and looked like a presage of some dire catastrophe.

"Bah! you are annoyed because they sang a requiem over 'les enfants morts nés,' as the Mississippians call your new écus," laughed the Regent. A week at the Bastille will be punishment enough for the offence."

The Regent's injunctions were of course obeyed, and after a week's confinement, the prisoners were liberated.

III.

M. DE MACHAULT.

About this time the public were greatly alarmed by a series of crimes, the perpetrators of which could not be discovered. The frequency and extraordinary nature of these crimes created the utmost consternation among the wealthy brokers and jobbers, and representations having been made to Law, he sent for M. de Machault, lieutenant-general of police, to confer with him on the subject.

"No doubt some terrible crimes have lately been committed, monseigneur," said the lieutenant-general, in reply to Law's inquiries, "and the perpetrators have hitherto baffled our vigilance, but as we shall redouble our efforts, they cannot escape us long. Last night a dreadful deed was committed, of which you may not have heard. A certain Madame Dupin received yesterday three hundred thousand livres in billets de banque from M. Tourton, the banker in the Rue Quincampoix. Nothing more was heard of her till this morning, when at an early hour a hired carriage was found by the watch, upset, and without horses or driver, near the walls of the Temple. On searching the vehicle, the watch discovered, to their horror, a sack filled with the mutilated body of a woman. It was completely hacked in pieces. I have since ascertained that the victim was Madame Dupin. This crime corresponds with another, perpetrated only a few days ago, showing that the same hand has been at work in both cases. General Bragousse sent his valet to a broker in the Rue Quincampoix to negotiate a hundred thousand shares. The man disappeared, and the general believed he had decamped with the money. But it was not so. The body of the unfortunate valet was found, hacked in pieces, beneath the Pont Royal. That many other crimes of a similar nature must have been committed, is certain, since a quantity of legs and arms, with other fragments of persons who have been assassinated, have been dragged out of the Seine. Corpses are found daily in the river, but it is difficult to tell whether the unfortunates have committed suicide or died by violence."

"A frightful state of things," remarked Law. "Public safety requires that these assassins should be discovered, and a terrible example made of them."

"All suspected persons are carefully watched," replied Machault, "and I have no doubt we shall secure the miscreants before long. We are aware that the notorious Cartouche is now in Paris, and these audacious crimes seem traceable to him. But society is shockingly demoralised. Robberies are constantly being committed by young libertines of good family. Many of these brigands have been arrested, but their places are quickly filled up by others. At this moment, were we to go to the Rue Quincampoix, I could point out to you a hundred richly-dressed galliards, apparently young men of fashion, who are really cheats and pickpockets."

"The street must be cleared of such villains, or it will not be safe to do business within it," observed Law.

"I intend to clear it," replied the lieutenant-general. "But I do not wish to cause alarm. I may mention to you, monseigneur, that an atrocious design has been conceived by these libertines, which, were it put into execution, would astound all Paris. It is this. They have planned to form themselves into bands—each band to have a leader. Their design is to secure the guard stationed at the gates of the Rue Quincampoix, and then, sword in hand, fall upon the stock-jobbers, and rifle them of their porte-feuilles. In this way, they calculate upon an immense booty."

"I trust they will not have an opportunity of executing the atrocious design," observed Law.

"Fear nothing, monseigneur. The contrivers of the scheme are under surveillance. You may remember that the Comte de Horn, with Captain de Mille and the Chevalier D'Etampes, were sent to the Bastille for interrupting the interment of the procureur Nigon."

"I perfectly recollect the scandalous occurrence," replied Law. "But what of those young men? Surely they are not implicated in the criminal design you have alluded to?"

"I have reason to believe the plan was contrived by one of them," replied Machault. "They have just been liberated from the Bastille, but I suspect it will not be long before they are sent back again."

"Strict watch ought to be kept over them,"

said Law. "There never was a time when it was more necessary for the police to be vigilant than at present."

"You shall have no cause for complaint, monseigneur," returned the lieutenant-general. "If any further discoveries are made, I will not fail to report them to you."

So saying, he bowed and took his leave.

IV.

M. LACROIX.

On their liberation from the Bastille, the Comte de Horn and his companions proceeded to the Fair of Saint-Germain, where they indulged themselves in a revel which nearly exhausted their funds. On examining their porte-feuilles next morning, they found they had only a few hundred livres left. Worse than all, they owed a large bill to the landlord of the Hôtel de Flandre, where they lodged, and he threatened them with imprisonment if it was not paid. In this emergency, De Mille again undertook to supply them with funds, and at once proceeded to the Hôtel Mazarin, where he found his father in a bureau with several clerks.

"Permit me a word with you in private, M. Laborde," he said.

"I am busy, sir, and cannot attend to you," returned his father, scarcely noticing him. "Come at some other time."

"My business cannot be delayed," returned De Mille. "I have something important to say to you."

Thinking it might be difficult to get rid of him without a scene, which he was anxious, if possible, to avoid, Laborde, with evident reluctance, led the way to an inner room.

"Now, sir, what is it?" he demanded, closing the door. "The old story, eh?—money!"

"Ay, money, father," replied De Mille. "I am in a terrible fix, or I wouldn't apply to you. Give me a hundred thousand livres, and dictate your own terms. Bid me leave Paris, and I go."

"I have no reliance whatever on your promises, sir, and, apparently, you pay little heed to what I say to you. I have told you I will give you no more money, and I do not mean to break my word."

"Then I shall commit some desperate action, and you will be responsible for it."

"That threat does not trouble me," rejoined Laborde. "I care not what becomes of you."

"But you care for your own reputation. If I am driven to crime, you will be dishonoured. You are rich, and won't feel the loss of the paltry sum I ask of you. It will profit you more to save your son from ruin than to accumulate wealth in your coffers."

"I am not to be moved by either supplication or threats," rejoined his father, sternly. "You shall have no further assistance from me."

"Is this your determination, sir?" said De Mille, regarding him fiercely.

"It is my fixed determination," rejoined Laborde.

"Very well, then," said his son. "When you next hear of me, you may, perhaps, regret it."

And he quitted the room.

Scarcely was he gone, than his father, struck by his manner, relented, and followed him, with the intention of calling him back. But he had already quitted the bureau. While Laborde was reflecting upon the course he ought to take, he cast his eyes upon a respectable-looking, middle-aged man, who was seated in the bureau. This was a broker named Lacroix. At the sight of him an idea occurred to Laborde.

"M. Lacroix," he said, "did you notice the person who has just gone out?"

"I did, sir," replied Lacroix. "It is Captain de Mille. I have often seen him with the Comte de Horn and the Chevalier D'Etampes in the Rue Quincampoix."

"Step into my room for a moment," said Laborde. And, as the broker followed him into the chamber, he shut the door, and went on: "I have something for you to do, Lacroix. It is a delicate task that I desire you to fulfil. Between ourselves, Captain de Mille is in difficulties, and I want to aid him, though I do not wish to appear in the matter. Take this porte-feuille. It contains a hundred and fifty thousand livres in billets de banque. Go to the Rue Quincampoix, and, if you see Captain de Mille, accost him, and inquire if he has any actions to sell. I know he has none, but he will, no doubt, procure the shares from some other broker. But mind this. He is to make five thousand livres by the transaction. You understand?"

"Perfectly, sir," replied Lacroix. "And I will faithfully carry out your instructions."

And he departed on his errand. In about an hour, he returned to inform his employer that he had been successful.

"I have seen Captain de Mille and his friends," he said, "and all has gone as you would have it. They have agreed to sell me twenty-five shares. I am to meet them to-morrow morning at seven o'clock at the Epée de Bois, in the Ruelle de Venise, to conclude the affair."

"You have managed it excellently," replied Laborde. "But don't forget my instructions. Calculate the price so that Captain de Mille can make five thousand livres."

"It shall be done," replied Lacroix.

V.

THE EPÉE DE BOIS.

"CHANCE seems to have thrown the very man we want into our hands," said De Mille to his friends, after Lacroix had left them. "We must get possession of his porte-feuille to-morrow morning."

"I am ready for anything," said De Horn.

"And so am I," said D'Etampes. "But let us talk the matter over before we decide. It is useless to commit a crime if it can be avoided."

"Meantime, let us have something to drink," said De Horn.

This being agreed to, they entered the Hôtel de Louisiane and called for a bottle of cognac, which being set before them by Rossignol, they each swallowed a large glass of the spirit.

"Now," said De Mille, "we can look our position fairly in the face. I have already explained to you that I have failed to obtain money in the quarter I expected. We can only muster three hundred livres amongst us, barely sufficient for our expenses to-night. To-morrow, we shall be without a sou."

"Unless my brother, Prince Maximilian, to whom I have written in very urgent terms, should send me a remittance," remarked the Comte de Horn; "but I confess I don't expect it."

"At all events, it won't do to calculate upon the chance," said De Mille. "We cannot afford to wait. Unless we can pay a hundred thousand livres to the landlord of our hotel to-morrow, we shall be clapped in prison, that is certain. We must have the money."

"We are all agreed upon that point," said De Horn. "But how?"

"Take another glass of brandy," replied De Mille, filling the count's glass, "and I'll tell you. To-morrow morning we must take that man's portfolio from him."

"But he is not likely to yield it up without a struggle," remarked De Horn.

"We must prevent the struggle—poniard him, and then take his porte-feuille."

"I am not squeamish," said D'Etampes. "I don't mind robbing the man, but assassination is not to my taste."

"What say you, De Horn?" demanded De Mille. "Do you agree to the plan?"

"I do," replied the count. "D'Etampes can keep watch outside the room while the deed is done. Have you a poniard, De Mille?"

"No," replied the other. "Let us go and procure weapons. There is a cutler on the Pont-

Neuf who will serve our turn. On the way, we can talk over the plan."

Proceeding to the Pont-Neuf, they procured the weapons they required; after which they went to the Fair of Saint-Germain, where they passed the night in riot, till, overcome by their potations, they fell asleep in their chairs. Well would it have been if they could have slept on, but at an early hour De Mille shook off his slumbers, and, rousing De Horn, said to him, in a low voice:

"It is nearly six o'clock. Our appointment is for seven. If we are not punctual, we may lose our man."

"I thought the deed was done," replied De Horn, with a ghastly look. "I have been dreaming of a dreadful struggle."

"You have had a nightmare, that is all," rejoined De Mille.

And he then proceeded to waken D'Etampes.

"I wish you would leave me out of the business," said the latter, shuddering. "My courage fails me. I like the job less than ever, now."

"No, you must go with us," said De Mille, suspiciously. "Be yourself, and shake off this irresolution. The affair will soon be settled. Have you got your poniard?" he added, in a low voice, to De Horn.

"Ay, it is here," replied the other, touching his vest.

Sallying forth, they shaped their course to the Pont-Neuf, which they crossed, and then proceeding along the Quai de la Mégisserie, entered the Rue Saint Dénis.

By this time, the Comte de Horn and De Mille, whose nerves were of iron, had shaken off the effects of their nocturnal debauch, and marched along with vigorous step; but D'Etampes walked with unsteady gait, and his companions had frequently to stop for him. Though the appearance of all three betokened the disorders in which they had been indulging, there was nothing in the circumstance to excite surprise, since there were many other young men in the streets of equally dissolute look.

Turning into the Rue Aubry-le-Boucher, they passed through the grille, which had not been long opened, and entered the Rue Quincampoix.

Even at this early hour there were a good many persons in the street, and business had already commenced. Several brokers addressed the young men, offering them shares, but they took no heed, and, passing on, soon reached the Ruelle de Venise.

At the farther end of this blind alley, now known as the Impasse de Venise, stood the Epée de Bois, a third-rate cabaret, very inferior to the taverns in the Rue Quincampoix, and only frequented by the lower order of Mississippians. De Mille had selected it as a place of rendezvous, because neither he nor his associates were known at the house.

Plunging into the alley, where there was no

crowd to impede their progress, they soon reached the Epée de Bois, but Lacroix had not yet arrived.

Two persons, however, were standing at the door of the cabaret, and in these they recognised the Irishmen whom they had fleeced some months before. The rencontre was by no means agreeable, but they made the best of it, and returned the salutations addressed to them by the Hibernians, whose appearance betokened a decided change of fortune for the worse. By this time the Irishmen had managed to acquire a sufficient knowledge of the French language to make themselves understood, and they were exchanging a few words with De Horn and the others, when Lacroix was seen coming down the alley. On this, De Mille went to meet him.

"I hope I have not kept you waiting, sir?" said Lacroix.

"Pray make no apologies, sir," replied De

Mille. "We are rather before our time. But let us go into the house, and settle our affair."

"Willingly, sir," replied Lacroix. "I am all ready for you."

"I hope you haven't forgotten your porte-feuille, M. Lacroix," remarked De Mille, forcing a laugh.

"Rest easy, sir; it is here," replied Lacroix, touching his breast.

They then entered the cabaret, and summoning the garçon, De Mille ordered a private room. As the garçon was conducting them to a chamber on the first floor, they again encountered the Irishmen, who told them they were lodging in the cabaret, on the second floor, and should be happy to see them when they had done their business. Internally execrating them, De Mille promised to come up to their room, and to his great relief they went away.

The party were then shown into a meanly-furnished chamber by the garçon, when De Horn addressed him thus: "We have an important negotiation to arrange with this gentleman, and do not desire to be interrupted. Prepare a good breakfast — a very good breakfast, d'ye hear, garçon? but don't serve it till we ring the bell."

"Monsieur may depend he shall have an excellent déjeûner," replied the garçon.

"Mind!" cried De Mille, "we are on no account to be interrupted."

The garçon nodded, and as soon as he was gone, Lacroix began to make calculations upon a piece of paper.

At a sign from De Mille, D'Etampes then quitted the room, and stationed himself on the stairs outside the door.

The moment for action had now arrived, and the assassins, who had been closely watching their victim, approached him.

"I see you are making your calculations, M. Lacroix," said De Mille. "Have you sufficient funds to pay us for twenty-five shares at sixteen thousand livres each?"

"I will tell you in a moment," said Lacroix. "I have a proposition to make to you in reference to the shares, which I am persuaded will meet with your approval. But first allow me to finish my calculation."

While he was thus occupied, De Mille leaned over his shoulder, and suddenly seizing the two corners of the cloth with which the table was covered, twisted the linen round the head of Lacroix so tightly as to prevent him crying out, while at the same moment De Horn, who was standing near, poniard in hand, plunged the weapon three or four times into the breast of the unfortunate man.

Notwithstanding all the efforts of the assassins to stifle the cries of their wretched victim, they could not prevent the escape of some fearful groans. These appalling sounds, coupled with the trampling of feet and the fall of several articles upset in the desperate struggle, reached the ears of Terry, who was in the room above, and listening attentively, he became convinced that some terrible deed was being enacted.

"Whist! Pat," he cried to his companion, who was changing a portion of his attire in an inner chamber. "D'ye hear them groans? As shure as the world, there's murder goin' on in the room beneath us."

"Murder is it?" cried Pat, presenting himself at the door of communication between the rooms. "By my troth, that did sound very like a groan."

"Clap your ear to the plank, as I'm doin', and ye'll be quite sartin ov it," said Terry. "Saints presarve us! somebody's kilt," he added, as the sound of a heavy body falling on the floor was distinctly heard.

"Out wid ye, Terry! and see wot's the matter, cried Pat. "Alarm the house. I'll be wid ye in a twinklin'."

Terry did not require a second bidding, but rushed out. On reaching the stairs, he perceived D'Etampes standing as sentinel at the door of the chamber in which the foul deed was being enacted. The blanched features and attitude of the wretch excited Terry's suspicions, and he determined to seize him. D'Etampes, however, did not wait for the other's approach, but, feeling certain that the alarm would be instantly given, hurried down stairs, and made good his retreat. Instead of following him, Terry stopped at the door of the fatal chamber, and peering through a crevice in it, beheld a sight that froze the blood in his veins.

The body of the unfortunate Lacroix was lying on the floor bathed in blood. Beside it stood De Horn, who was cleansing his poniard from its ruddy stains with a napkin, ever and anon glancing at his prostrate victim. De Mille, who seemed almost unconcerned at the atrocious deed, had possessed himself of the porte-feuille, and was feasting his greedy eyes with its contents. Little did he think that the porte-feuille was from his own father, and might have been obtained without bloodshed.

So horrified was Terry by the dreadful spectacle that met his gaze, that for a moment or two he could not stir. Rousing himself at last, he noticed that the key was in the lock, upon which he quickly fastened the door, and then flew down stairs to give the alarm.

The grating of the key in the lock startled the two assassins. Throwing down his poniard, De Horn sprang to the door and found it fastened. At that moment he heard the cry of the Irishman.

"Perdition!" he exclaimed. "The alarm has been given."

Even at this terrible conjuncture, De Mille preserved his coolness, and thrusting the porte-feuille, for which he had bartered his soul, into his breast, rushed to the window and threw it open.

On looking out, he saw that by means of certain projections in the timber of which the house was constructed descent was practicable, and, as luck would have it, there was no one at the moment in that part of the alley.

"Saved!" he cried. "We can get down here."

"Lose not a moment," cried De Horn, who was close behind him. "I hear them on the stairs."

De Mille then got through the window, and being very light and active, quickly reached a brow post, whence he let himself drop to the ground, but in the fall, which was from too great a height, he sprained his ankle severely. De Horn was more fortunate, and reached the ground in safety. Regardless of his companion, who limped after him, De Horn ran towards the Rue Quincampoix, and plunging into the crowd, which by this time had considerably augmented, disappeared.

Meantime, Terry, accompanied by the tavern-keeper and a couple of garçons, burst into the room which the assassins had just quitted. While the others were transfixed by the ghastly spectacle presented to their gaze, Terry rushed to the open window and caught sight of De Mille, who, unable to proceed farther, was seeking refuge in a doorway.

"There's one ov 'em! I see him!" cried Terry. "Come wid me, Pat," he added to his comrade. "We'll have him in less than no time!"

Caught in his retreat by the two Irishmen, De Mille was speedily overpowered, and being dragged back to the cabaret, was taken to the chamber of death and confronted with his victim. It was impossible for him to deny his guilt, and he did not attempt it. The porte-feuille was found upon him, and his laced ruffles and coat-sleeves were stained with blood.

VI.

THE PORTER OF THE HALLE.

MEANTIME, the alarm had been given by the garçons of the cabaret, and in an incredibly short space of time it was known by every one in the Rue Quincampoix that a frightful assassination had been committed by some young men of rank at the Epée de Bois, in the Ruelle de Venise.

The gates at the Rue Aubry-le-Boucher and the Rue-aux-Ours were closed, and no one was allowed by the guard to pass through without strict investigation. But these precautions were taken too late, as far as D'Etampes was concerned. Long before the alarm was given he was out of the Rue Quincampoix, and, springing into a hired coach, drove with all possible expedition to the Hôtel de Flandre, where he secured a few portable effects, and then quitted Paris. Nor was he afterwards taken, but passed the remainder of his days in the Dutch Indies, under the name of Grandpré.

The Comte de Horn managed to elude the vigilance of the corps-de-garde stationed at the grille of the Rue Aubry-le-Boucher, but his habiliments being torn, and stained with blood, he did not dare to proceed along the Rue Saint Denis, but hurried towards the Halle, with the intention of entering some obscure cabaret in that quarter.

The market was then at its height, and he might have escaped detection, had not his scared looks and disordered attire attracted the attention of a sturdy porter, who caught hold of him and stopped him.

"Hola, monsieur!" cried this personage, detaining him in his rough gripe. "What's the matter? From the blood upon your shirt and sleeves, I judge you have been engaged in a desperate fray. Have you been fighting with some of the canaille in the Halle? You look like a person of quality. Can I serve you?"

"I am infinitely obliged to you, my good friend," replied De Horn, terrified by the detention. "I am, as you conjecture, a person of condition. The blood you see upon my dress is my own. I have been set upon by ruffians in a tavern hard by, and deem myself lucky in escaping with life."

"Milles diables!" exclaimed the porter. "This is a case for the commissary of police. Allons, monsieur. I'll conduct you to the office."

"You are very obliging, my friend, but I needn't trouble you to go with me," replied De Horn. "Direct me to the office—that will suffice."

"Bah! it's no trouble at all. The office is

close at hand—in the Rue Aubry-le-Boucher. I know M. Regnard, the commissary, very well. I'll introduce you to him."

"But there is no sort of necessity, I tell you," said De Horn, scarcely able to conceal his uneasiness. "If the office is in the Rue Aubry-le-Boucher I can easily find it."

"You had better have me with you, or you will be insulted by the dames de la Halle," rejoined the porter. "Some of 'em, I see, are eyeing you sharply already."

Finding he could not get rid of his tormentor without exciting suspicion, De Horn suffered himself to be conducted to the Rue Aubry-le-Boucher, the porter keeping close to his side all the way, so that flight was impossible.

On arriving at the police-office, they were at once ushered into the presence of M. Regnard, the commissary, who listened attentively to De Horn's tale. Before, however, the wretched young man had concluded his recital, a tumult was heard in the outer room, and an officer rushed in to say that a frightful assassination had just been committed at the Epée de Bois, in the Ruelle de Venise, by two young seigneurs, of whom one was taken, but the other had escaped.

"Then this is the man you want!—this is the second assassin!" cried the porter, pointing to De Horn, whose looks and demeanour proclaimed his guilt. "The moment I clapped eyes upon him I said to myself that man is an assassin, and I was determined not to let him go, but to bring him to you, M. le Commissaire. He came quietly enough, I must say; but I would have brought him by force if he had resisted."

"You have done well, Bertrand," said Regnard, approvingly; "and if, as I suspect, this should turn out to be the man, you shall be handsomely rewarded."

"I want no reward for bringing an assassin to justice," replied Bertrand. "I have merely acted like a good citizen."

At a sign from the commissary, two more officers were called in, and De Horn was arrested. On being interrogated, he did not seek to disguise his name and rank, expecting that when he stated that he belonged to the highest ranks of the nobility, that he was the younger brother of a Prince of the Pays Bas, a relative of the Emperor of Germany, of the Princess Palatine, and of the Regent himself, M. Regnard would order his release. But in this expectation he was deceived. The announcement merely let the commissary know that this was one of the young seigneurs about whom he had previously received instructions from his chief, M. de Machault. So he ordered a detachment of archers to be sent for, and as soon as they arrived took the prisoner to the Epée de Bois.

The crowd in the Rue Quincampoix was in an extraordinarily excited and tumultuous state. Execrations and menaces greeted the prisoner as he passed along, and but for the strong guard that surrounded him, he might have fared ill.

The Ruelle de Venise was blocked up, but a passage being cleared through the throng, De Horn was taken into the cabaret, and led to the room in which the body of his victim was still lying. Here he found his guilty associate, who cast one look at him as he was brought in, but not a word passed between them.

In the room, seated at the table, and writing notes, was M. de Machault. He had been hastily summoned, and, ever since his arrival, had been occupied in examining the witnesses, the chief of whom were the two Irishmen, the tavern-keeper, and the garçon. By these witnesses De Mille's guilt had already been established, and their evidence in regard to De Horn's participation in the crime was equally conclusive.

The inquiry did not last long. Satisfied of the guilt of both parties, M. de Machault ordered them to be taken to the Grand Châtelet, and they were escorted thither by the archers, the same fearful demonstrations from the crowd accompanying them as had attended De Horn on his way to the Epée de Bois. The prisoners were not allowed to have any discourse together, but were lodged in separate dungeons.

After sending the prisoners to the Grand Châtelet, M. de Machault repaired to the Hôtel Law, where he had an interview with the comptroller-general. He subsequently went to the Palais Royal, to learn the Regent's pleasure respecting the Comte de Horn, and was told that justice must take its course. Shortly afterwards, Law had an audience of the Regent, and in consequence of the comptroller-general's representations, an order was sent by the Regent to the presiding judge of the court of the Grand Châtelet, enjoining that the two assassins, having been taken flagrante delicto, should be brought to trial without delay. In obedience to this mandate, on the very next day the process commenced.

By this time De Horn had fully recovered his

confidence, persuading himself that he had interest enough to save him from the penalty of his crime, and, though De Mille did not entertain the same conviction, his natural audacity stood him in good stead, and he betrayed no misgiving as to the result of the trial. In fact, the demeanour of both was marked with so much levity, and they seemed so utterly insensible of the enormity of the offence laid to their charge, as to excite the indignation and reprehension of the court.

After a long and patient examination, they were found guilty, and sentenced to be broken alive on the wheel in the Place de Grève, on the sixth day from that on which their crime had been committed. This terrible sentence did not produce much effect upon the prisoners, and for the simple reason that neither of them believed it would be carried into effect.

"Don't be cast down," whispered De Horn to his companion in crime. "This is mere form.

We are not destined to make a spectacle in the Place de Grève. My friends have promised to obtain us a pardon from the Regent."

They were then removed by the officers in attendance, and taken back to their dungeons.

VII.

HOW THE REGENT REFUSED TO COMMUTE THE COMTE DE HORN'S SENTENCE.

THE assassination of Lacroix created an extraordinary sensation throughout Paris. That such a daring crime could be committed in the open day, in a public cabaret, within a few yards of the crowded Rue Quincampoix, where the cries of the victim might have been heard, filled all the speculators with alarm. Business was almost at a standstill in the Rue Quincampoix. The brokers were uneasy in their bureaux; the bankers and money-lenders shut up their counters; and the Mississippians did not dare to bring their porte-feuilles with them. Many young men who had been known to associate with De Horn and the others were regarded with suspicion.

Though a crime of this nature was as abhorrent to the feelings of the nobility as to those of all other classes of society, the condemnation of the Comte de Horn to the death of a common felon was felt as a blow to the whole order. Efforts had been made to divert the course of justice and screen the perpetrators of the crime, but such was the promptitude with which they were brought to trial, that these efforts were defeated. The court had been crowded with persons of the highest rank, and amongst them were the Duc de Chatillon, the Duc d'Aremberg, the Prince de Robecq-Montmorency, and the Maréchal d'Isinghien, all four near relatives of the Comte de Horn, and it was the presence of these personages that made the unfortunate young man so confident of escape. To the proud nobles themselves the sentence passed upon their dishonoured relative was a degradation which they could not brook, and their feelings were shared by the other nobles present. On leaving the court, they held a conference together, and it was resolved that the Prince de Montmorency and the other connexions of the house of Horn should see the Regent without delay, and procure from his highness either the pardon of their unfortunate relative, or a commutation of the sentence.

Their intentions being reported to Law, he obtained an audience of the Regent at an early hour on the following day, and implored his highness not to yield to any solicitations that might be made him to spare the assassins, as the atrocious nature of the crime imperatively demanded that the sentence should be carried out. "The greatest consternation has been caused among all the holders of billets de banque," he said, "and a terrible example must be made of the offenders, to reassure them. Unless the Comte de Horn and his associate are executed, there will no longer be any security for moneyed men in Paris. I pray your highness, therefore, to be inflexible."

"I feel with you," said the Regent. "Such a crime as this must not pass unpunished. I will turn a deaf ear to all the supplications addressed to me—no matter by whom."

Law had not been gone long, when, as had been foreseen, the Prince de Montmorency, the Ducs de Chatillon and D'Aremberg, with the Maréchal d'Isinghien, besought an interview with the Regent, and were at once admitted.

The Regent received them with great consideration, evincing by his manner the sympathy he felt for them.

"We have come," said the Prince de Montmorency, "as supplicants to your highness in behalf of our unhappy kinsman, the Comte de Horn. We do not for a moment attempt to extenuate the crime he has committed. It is of the darkest dye, and deserves the severest punishment.

If the consequences fell only upon his own head, we would not interpose between him and justice. Nay, if he were doomed to die by the axe, no word of remonstrance should be heard from us. Two of his ancestors died so. Philippe, Comte de Horn, was beheaded by the Duke of Alva in 1568, and two years later, Comte Floris de Horn was put to death in like manner by Philip II. of Spain. Their deaths brought no dishonour to the house. But if Comte Antoine de Horn should die the felon's death to which he has been adjudged, an ineffaceable stain will be cast on every branch of his illustrious house. There is scarcely a noble family in the Pays Bas but the house of Horn is allied with it. Shall dishonour be brought upon all these houses? Shall it be told to the Comte Maximilien, the proudest and most chivalrous of men, that his brother has been broken on the wheel? Shall it be told to the Emperor of Germany that a member of his royal house has died this shameful death? Even the Princess Palatine and your highness yourself will be touched by it."

"Eh bien!" cried the Regent, "I will share the opprobrium with you all. That ought to be a consolation to the other relatives."

"I cannot believe, monseigneur, that you will inflict this indelible disgrace upon a house so illustrious and so proudly allied,' said the Maréchal d'Isinghien. "Your highness may not be aware that if Comte Antoine de Horn should be broken on the wheel, his family will be rendered infamous for three generations. Besides the shame they will have to endure, no male can become an abbé or bishop, no female a canoness. At this very moment the sister of the unhappy Antoine is about to enter a convent, but she cannot do so if her brother dies this infamous death. For her sake—for the sake of her brother Prince Maximilien—for the sake of us all—commute this miserable young man's sentence to decapitation.

I ask no further grace, but I beseech you to save a noble house from dishonour."

"It is not the mode of death that degrades, but the offence," replied the Regent.

> "La crime fait la honte, et non pas l'échafaud.

The Comte de Horn has committed a felon's act, and must die a felon's death. I cannot—will not commute his punishment."

"I grieve to hear your highness say so," said the Duc d'Aremberg, sternly. "By this severity you will make enemies of all the nobles of the Pays Bas and Germany, who will feel themselves outraged. The Emperor would have passed no such sentence."

"I will go further than that," said Montmorency, boldly. "The Emperor will be justly indignant that one of his house should be executed like a felon."

"I cannot help his anger," said the Regent, impatiently. "If I make all the nobles of the Pays

Bas, and all those of Germany, my mortal foes, I will not pervert justice."

"Your nobility look to you as the guardian of their privileges, monseigneur," said the Duc de Chatillon. "In your hands their honour ought to remain unsullied. You are yielding to the people, who clamour that the high birth of the Comte de Horn will shield him from the consequences of his crime; and the concession you are making will react upon the throne. We know the pressure that has been brought to bear upon your highness. We know that the comptroller-general has stated that an example must be made. But we beseech you to listen to our supplications, not to him. If this ignominious sentence is carried out, be assured we shall never forgive M. Law for the injury inflicted upon us."

"Have you done, messieurs?" demanded the Regent, coldly.

"We have," replied Montmorency, sternly. "And we only regret that we should have troubled your highness at all. We are persuaded you will rue this step."

"I do not think so," returned the Regent. "But I shall not shrink from the consequences, be they what they may. I am sorry I cannot listen to your prayers—that is impossible. But is there any other grace I can show you? Perhaps you may desire to visit your unhappy kinsman in his prison? If so, you shall have permission to do so."

There was a certain significance in the tone in which this proposition was made, that conveyed more than the words implied, and after the supplicants had conferred a moment together, the Prince de Montmorency said:

"The Maréchal d'Isinghien and myself will avail ourselves of your highness's permission to visit the prisoner."

"You will do well," rejoined the Regent. "Perhaps you may be able to reconcile him to his doom."

"We will try," said Montmorency.

And bowing profoundly, the whole party took their departure.

As soon as they were gone, Nocé, who had been standing at the back of the cabinet, came forward.

"Your highness has displayed more firmness than I expected," he remarked.

"I cannot commute De Horn's sentence," replied the Regent. "I would rather displease the nobles than the people. I gave Montmorency a hint, and I hope he will act upon it."

"I am sure he will," said Nocé. "But I doubt whether De Horn has the courage to save himself from this ignominious death. Your highness must admit I am a good physiognomist. I foretold that this young man would come to a violent end."

"I begin to think your prediction will be fulfilled," replied the Regent.

VIII.

HOW THE PRINCE DE MONTMORENCY AND THE MARÉCHAL D'ISINGHIEN HAD AN INTERVIEW WITH THE COMTE DE HORN IN THE GRAND CHATELET.

LATER on in the day, and provided with a warrant from the Regent, the Prince de Montmorency and the Maréchal d'Isinghien repaired to the Grand Châtelet, in the dungeons of which their unhappy kinsman was bestowed.

In these prisons, which were among the strongest in Paris, many tragical events occurred at the time of the League, and during the faction of the Armagnacs. Some of the dungeons were horrible places, as may be inferred from their names—les Chaines, la Fosse, le Puits, les Oubliettes, and les Boucheries. Prisoners were lowered into "le Puits," which was knee-deep in water, in the way that a bucket is let down into a well. In the lowest depths of the Grand Châtelet there was a frightful hole called "Fin d'aise," in which a prisoner could neither stand upright nor sit down. These dungeons were demolished at the commencement of the present century.

But it was not in any of the horrible places just referred to that the Comte de Horn and Captain de Mille were confined. The cells allotted to both were large and airy—that in which De Horn was placed being denominated "le Paradis," while De Mille was lodged in "la Gloriette."

The high rank of the visitors, and the order which they brought from the Regent, ensured them attention from the governor, M. Dartaguiette, who conducted them in person to the dungeon wherein their relative was confined, assuring them it was the best in the Châtelet, and as good as any chamber in the Bastille. After ushering them into the cell, M. Dartaguiette retired and left them alone with the prisoner—placing a gaoler outside the door. On their entrance, De Horn, who was seated at a little table, started joyfully to his feet, but their looks struck him with dismay.

"Have you brought me a pardon?" he inquired.

"You must prepare for the worst," replied Montmorency. "The Regent is inexorable. We have not asked for a pardon, but merely for a commutation of your sentence to death by the axe. But this his highness refuses."

"Must I, then, die?" almost shrieked De Horn.

"Undoubtedly," rejoined D'Isinghien. "And, what is more, you deserve death."

"Ah! you have been false to me!" cried De Horn. "You have not besought the Regent to spare me, but to put me to death. You are traitors. But I will find others who will reach his highness."

"Do not delude yourself by the idle expectation," said Montmorency, sternly. "I tell you the Regent is inexorable. You have committed an atrocious crime, for which you deserve the death to which you are adjudged, and it is only because the manner of your execution will bring infamy upon the prince your brother, upon the princess your sister, and upon all connected with your house, that we have interceded for you."

For a few minutes De Horn covered his face with his hands, and remained speechless. With quivering lips, and in broken accents, he then cried,

"Save me!—oh, save me from this infamous death!"

"There is only this means of escape," rejoined Montmorency, giving him a small phial.

"What is this?" cried De Horn. "Poison?"

"Drain that phial, and you will escape an ignominious death, and save your family from infamy," said D'Isinghien. "Our errand is done."

"Stay!" cried De Horn. "Take back the

phial. I will not die thus. I distrust you. You want to get rid of me. The Regent will never allow his own kinsman to be executed."

"Indulge no such hope," rejoined Montmorency. "Your fate is the wheel, unless you avoid it by the means we have just offered you."

"I cannot do it!" cried De Horn, thrusting the phial into Montmorency's hands.

"What!" exclaimed the prince, contemptuously. "Are you of such a craven nature that you fear death? Would you bring infamy upon your illustrious house and all its connexions? Shame on you!—shame on you!"

"But I shall not die!" cried the miserable young man. "The Regent will pardon me."

"Madman! you have no alternative but poison or a felon's death!" rejoined Montmorency. "Since you elect the latter, we have no further business here. You will not see us again."

And he turned his back upon him.

"You are the reproach of a noble race, and

are only worthy to die upon the wheel," cried D'Isinghien, regarding him with abhorrence.

Then, calling to the gaoler to open the door, they quitted the cell, leaving De Horn completely prostrated.

IX.

OF THE LAST INTERVIEW BETWEEN LABORDE AND HIS SON.

TERRIBLE was the effect produced upon Laborde by the intelligence that Lacroix had been barbarously assassinated. How could he do otherwise than charge himself with being the cause of the unfortunate man's destruction! A fit seized him, and he fell down insensible. Medical assistance being quickly procured by old Delmace, who was with him at the time, and who, in fact, had brought him the dreadful news, Laborde was saved from the consequences of the attack, but for two days his life was despaired of, and, during the whole of that time, he continued delirious.

On the morning of the third day an improvement took place. Having slept for a few hours, he awoke refreshed, and the cloud that had obscured his mind had partially cleared away. The first object his gaze rested upon was his daughter, who was seated by his couch, watching over him, while at a little distance stood old Delmace. Though Laborde's faculties were still in a confused state, he was sensible that a great change had taken place in Colombe's looks, and that her countenance bore traces of deep mental anguish.

"What is the matter with you, my child?" he inquired, in feeble tones. "What has happened?"

"Do not ask me, father," she rejoined. "You have been ill. Do you feel better?"

"Yes, I am better—much better," he rejoined. "But my head is still bewildered. I know some dire calamity has occurred. Don't keep it from me."

Colombe made no reply, but turned away to hide her tears. All at once the dreadful truth rushed upon Laborde, and, raising himself, he called out, in a voice that terrified both his daughter and old Delmace, the latter of whom rushed towards the bed.

"Your precautions are in vain. The fiends are yelling in my ears that I am the father of an assassin."

"Be calm, sir—be calm, I implore you," said Delmace, with difficulty restraining him. "For your daughter's sake be calm. You know not what she has endured. Be thankful to Heaven, sir, that if you have an evil son, who has caused you nothing but grief and shame, you have the best of daughters. Mademoiselle Colombe is an angel. She has been watching by you for two whole days and nights—ever since your attack."

"You are right, Delmace," said Laborde, upon

whom his old servant's words produced an instantaneous effect; "Colombe is an angel of goodness, and I ought to be grateful to Heaven for bestowing such a daughter upon me. I have treated you unkindly, my child," he added, taking her hand, "but if I am spared, I will make amends."

"Oh! do not think of me, dear father," she said. "Guilty as Raoul is, you must still think of him. Are you able to bear the afflicting news I have to tell you?"

"I am," replied Laborde. "I would rather hear the worst, however painful it may be, than be kept in suspense. Does my wretched son yet live?"

"He does," replied Colombe; "but he has been tried, and condemned to—to——" She could not finish the sentence.

"He is doomed to be broken on the wheel," supplied Delmace. "Three days hence the terrible sentence will be carried into effect at the Place de Grève."

"Horror!" exclaimed Laborde, sinking back upon his couch with a groan.

"You have said too much, Delmace," cried Colombe, reproachfully. "You have killed him by this intelligence."

"Oh! no, no. I can bear it," said Laborde. "I myself am not free from guilt in this dreadful affair."

"You, father—impossible!" exclaimed Colombe.

"Your brain is wandering, sir," said Delmace.

"No, my mind is clear enough now," rejoined Laborde. "I tell you that I have been unwittingly instrumental in causing the assassination of poor Lacroix. I sent him to assist Raoul, and it was in executing my orders that he met his terrible fate."

"This is indeed a sad and strange complication of the affair," said Colombe, "but you need not reproach yourself for an act that was intended for the best. It may be a consolation to you to know that Raoul was tried under his assumed name of Laurent de Mille, and has not been recognised as your son."

"For me it matters not," rejoined Laborde. "I cannot hide from myself the consciousness that I am the father of an assassin. I can never hold up my head again. But with you, Colombe, the case is different; and on your account I rejoice that no discovery has been made."

"I have deemed it right to impart the terrible truth to M. Law and Lady Catherine," said Colombe. "And I need not tell you, you have their profound commiseration."

"For your sake, Colombe, I wish the truth could have been concealed even from them," cried Laborde.

"I have done with the world, father," she rejoined. "I shall hide my woes in a convent."

"No, no—not so," he rejoined. "I am rich. You shall marry Evelyn, and be happy."

"That cannot be now, father," she rejoined, sadly.

At this moment a tap was heard at the door, and the summons being answered by Delmace, the old man presently returned to say that M. Law was in the outer room.

"Shall I go to him, father?" asked Colombe.

"No; beg him to come in," said Laborde to Delmace. "I am quite strong enough to see him."

On his entrance, Law took the chair which Colombe ceded to him by her father's bed-side, and expressed the profound sympathy he felt for the unfortunate man, adding, "I would urge you, if you feel equal to the effort, at once to leave Paris, and go to my château of Guermande, where you can remain till you are perfectly recovered. My carriage shall convey you thither. Be advised by me, and go," he continued, seeing that Laborde hesitated. "Guermande, as you know, is only a few leagues from Paris, so that the journey will not fatigue you much. You will be better out of the way. Colombe," he added to her, "you must prepare your father for immediate departure."

"I will obey you, sir," replied Laborde. "I feel it is for the best—but I must see my unfortunate son before I go."

"On no account," said Law. "The interview will answer no good purpose, and will only give you unnecessary pain."

"I am his father, monseigneur," replied Laborde, "and, though he has caused me inconceivable misery, I cannot shut my heart to him. I know the enormity of his crime—I know he does not deserve mercy—but is there any hope for him?"

"None whatever," replied Law. "The sentence will infallibly be carried out. Therefore I urge you, for your own sake, and for your daughter's sake, to depart at once for Guermande, and not subject yourself to a needless trial of your feelings. Why do you not dissuade your father from the hazardous design, Colombe?"

"Because I think he ought to see my unhappy brother," she rejoined. "I will go with him to the prison."

Finding nothing less would content them, Law yielded, and said, "In an hour my carriage shall be here, and shall take you to the Grand Châtelet. I will send you an order for admittance to the prisoner. After you have had the interview you desire, you can proceed at once to Guermande, where I hope you will spend a few weeks."

"I do not think I have many weeks to live, monseigneur," replied Laborde; "but I thank you from the bottom of my heart for your consideration."

Pressing poor Laborde's hand kindly, Law then quitted the room.

In an hour, as arranged, the carriage arrived, and Laborde and his daughter being ready, they entered it, and were driven to the Grand Châtelet, where the order sent them, according to his promise, by Law procured them immediate admittance to the prisoner.

On their entrance into his cell, which was nearly as large as that assigned to his wretched associate, De Mille, as we shall still continue to call him, manifested some discomposure, but almost immediately recovered his self-possession.

Poor Laborde, however, was so overcome by the sight of his son, that he sank down upon the only seat which the cell contained, and for some moments could not utter a word.

"I hope you will pass the few days left you on earth in penitence and prayer, Raoul," said Colombe, "and seek to obtain pardon from your Supreme Judge. Begin by imploring forgiveness from your father, whom you have so deeply afflicted."

"I cannot bend the knee to any man now," rejoined De Mille, stubbornly. "But my father is the cause of this catastrophe. If he had given me the money I asked for, it would not have happened."

"I had a good motive for the refusal," replied Laborde, "but it was my intention to let you have the money. Learn, miserable wretch, that the unfortunate Lacroix, whom you so ruthlessly slew, was my agent, and charged by me to give you money. The portefeuille you snatched from him was mine—ay, mine! If you had waited a few minutes, you would have been spared this dreadful crime."

"I suppose I must believe what you tell me," replied his son, surprised by the information. "But how was I to guess that Lacroix was your agent? You should not have adopted this roundabout mode of assisting me. If you had given me the money at once, I should not now be here."

"Oh, Raoul! how shocked I am to find you in this impenitent condition," cried Colombe. "If you harden your heart thus, you will perish everlastingly."

"I am no hypocrite, Colombe," replied her brother, "and I will not feign a penitence I do not—cannot feel. I don't like to die. Life is sweet; and if my career were not cut short in this merciless manner, I might enjoy many years of pleasure."

"Pleasure!—always pleasure!" cried Colombe. "It is your insatiate love of pleasure that has destroyed you."

"Life is worth nothing without enjoyment," rejoined her brother. "I don't fear death. But the wheel is a horrible punishment. I have always been vain of my limbs, and don't desire to have them shattered. Have you brought me anything, Colombe?"

"Here is a devout book, which I pray you to peruse," she replied, giving him a small volume. "It will afford you consolation."

"I don't want that," he replied, tossing it aside disdainfully. Then, drawing near to her, he added, in a low voice, "Have you brought me anything to enable me to avoid the wheel?"

"No," she replied, shuddering. "Do you think I would furnish you with the means of self-destruction?"

"Why not?" he rejoined, almost fiercely. "It would be the kindest thing you could do for me. I would have thanked you if you had enabled me to avoid that horrible wheel. But since you have come empty-handed, you might have spared me the visit."

"Father, let us go," said Colombe. "We shall do no good here."

"Oh! my son! my son!" cried Laborde, in a voice of anguish. "I call upon you, at this supreme moment, to repent—so that you may yet be forgiven."

"Will not those cries move you?" said Colombe.

"No," replied her brother. "I will die as I have lived."

Laborde gazed at him for some moments in speechless anguish, but finding there were no signs of yielding, he called to the gaoler, and quitted the cell with his daughter.

"M. Law was right," he observed to Colombe. "I ought to have avoided this interview."

In less than three hours afterwards Laborde and his daughter arrived at the splendid Château de Guermande, near Lagny. But no new day dawned upon the unfortunate man. The interview with his guilty son had been too much for him. He had another fit that night, and expired in his daughter's arms.

X.

THE CURÉ DE SAINT PAUL.

THE hope of a pardon, to which the unhappy Comte de Horn obstinately clung, despite what had been said to him by his two noble kinsmen, was at last dispelled by Père Gueret, Curé de Saint Paul, who visited him in his cell on the afternoon of the following day.

"Your doom is sealed, my son," said the curé to him. "You have not many hours to live. Make the most, therefore, of the little time left you on earth. By full confession of your sins, by heartfelt penitence, and by earnest supplication, you may obtain forgiveness of Heaven. But here there is no longer any hope for you on earth."

For some time the wretched young man was in a state of great excitement, refusing to listen to Père Gueret's exhortations of the good curé, but at last, becoming calmer, he knelt down, and made his shrift, professing such profound contrition for his offences, that the good curé could not refuse him absolution.

Much comforted, De Horn then said to the priest,

"I deserve to die on the wheel, but I hope, out of consideration for my noble family, that the Regent, in his goodness, will accord me a less dishonourable death."

"I can hold out no hopes for you, my son," replied Père Gueret. "M. Law told me this morning that the Regent is inexorable. You must, therefore, resign yourself to your doom."

At the words, a mortal sickness seized De Horn. Alarmed by his appearance, the good curé aided him to a seat, and was about to summon the gaoler, when the prisoner stopped him, saying,

"It is only a momentary faintness. It will pass."

Damps broke out upon his brow, and relieved him, but his face was deadly white, and his very lips were bloodless.

"Tell me, good father," he gasped, fixing a haggard look upon the curé, "does one suffer much on the wheel?"

The curé regarded him compassionately, scarcely knowing how to reply, but at last said,

"If you are sincerely penitent, my son, Heaven will strengthen you to endure the pain. The penitent thief who suffered with our blessed Lord was supported on the cross. Call upon the blessed saints and martyrs in the hour of agony, and I doubt not you will be sustained. I shall be near you to the last, and will not cease to pray for your speedy deliverance."

With this the good man quitted the cell, and

proceeded to that of De Mille, with whom, however, he was less successful than he had been with the other prisoner. De Mille refused all spiritual assistance. At last the curé, incensed by his obstinacy, exclaimed,

"Miserable wretch! You will die unabsolved, and your soul will remain ever in torment. Very different from your conduct is that of the partner of your guilt. He has made his peace with Heaven."

"What! has the Comte de Horn surrendered himself into the hands of a priest?" cried De Mille, with a derisive laugh. "I did not deem him capable of such weakness."

"His weakness, as you profanely call it, will profit him more than your obstinacy," said the curé. "But, hardened as you are, I trust that your heart may yet be touched. I will pray that it may be so."

XI.

HOW A CHANGE WAS WROUGHT IN DE MILLE.

PÈRE GUERET had not long quitted the cell, when another person was introduced by the gaoler, who retired and left him with the prisoner. The new comer was Evelyn Harcourt.

"What brings you here, sir?" demanded De Mille, in a stern voice. "Do you come to mock me, or to gratify an idle curiosity?"

"I come at the instance of your afflicted sister," replied Evelyn.

"What sister?" cried De Mille, almost fiercely. "I have none. And if I had, I do not see what right you have to meddle with me and my family."

"The prevarication will answer no purpose," said Evelyn. "I know the truth. It is only at your sister's request that I have consented to come here. I bring news of your father."

"If you persist in calling Laborde my father, I cannot help it," rejoined De Mille. "But I acknowledge no relationship to him."

"The disclaimer is useless," said Evelyn. "Colombe has told me all."

"I am sorry for it," rejoined De Mille. "You are the very last person to whom the secret should have been confided. I hoped it might die with me, and then no harm would have been done to my family. But what news do you bring of my father?"

"Prepare yourself," said Evelyn, in a solemn voice. "He is dead."

"Dead!" almost shrieked De Mille. "Then I am a parricide. Oh, Heaven! the measure of my iniquities would not have been complete without this heinous crime."

"I will not disguise from you that the shock you have given your father has killed him," said Evelyn. "He died last night in the arms of his daughter, at the Château de Guermande, whence I have just returned."

"I am, indeed, a wretch unworthy to live," cried De Mille, horror-stricken. "Père Gueret told me just now that my heart would be touched —and so it is. I see the hand of Heaven in this. I now comprehend the magnitude of my offences, and will repent of them. But there is no hope for such a sinner as I am."

"There is always hope," said Evelyn. "Your father forgave you with his dying lips, and will intercede for you at the throne of Mercy. Make your peace with Heaven."

"I will strive to do so," rejoined the other, in broken accents. "Oh, Evelyn! I have been fatal to my family. My poor mother's heart was broken by my reckless conduct, and now I have destroyed my father. But let me not destroy Colombe. Do not cease to love her because she is my sister. No two human beings were ever more unlike in character than she and I—she all goodness—I the incarnation of evil. If I had listened to her admonitions I should not be here now—sullied by crime and filled with remorse. Forget, if you can, that such a wretch as Raoul Laborde ever existed, and let my name never be mentioned between you and Colombe. Say you will continue to love her, Evelyn. She will die if you abandon her."

"Fear nothing," replied Evelyn. "All the trials Colombe has endured have only tended to exalt her character in my eyes, and strengthen my affection for her."

"Oh! thanks for that assurance," cried De Mille. "Certain that the fatal influence I have exercised over both my parents will not attach to Colombe—certain she will be happy—I shall die content. Tell Colombe that her image will enable me to bear my punishment without a groan, and that my latest thoughts will be hers. And now farewell for ever, Evelyn! When you go forth, I pray you send Père Guenet to me. He will find me an altered man."

"It will console your sister in her deep affliction to hear of this change in you," said Evelyn. "Be assured she will not forget you in her prayers. Farewell for ever!"

And he quitted the cell.

Shortly afterwards Père Gueret again made his appearance. De Mille threw himself humbly and penitently at his feet, cleansed his bosom of its heavy load, and received absolution.

XII.

THE PLACE DE GRÈVE.

The day of execution arrived.

A vast concourse had assembled in the Place de Grève, where preparations had been made for the tragical drama about to be enacted. A large scaffold, draped with black, had been erected on the side of the place nearest the Hôtel de Ville; and on this scaffold were the two hideous machines to which the sufferers were to be attached. The dismal structure was guarded by a body of archers in their full equipments. The windows of every habitation commanding a view of the

Place de Grève were filled with spectators, and in front of the Hôtel de Ville was ranged a long line of carriages, sent thither by the noble relatives of the Comte de Horn; the coachmen and footmen being in mourning, as if they were in attendance upon a funeral. This was the only recognition of his rank shown to the unhappy young man. A guard of mounted mousquetaires placed in front of the carriages, protected them from the crowd.

The patience of the amateurs of sanguinary exhibitions worthy of ancient Rome was severely tried. They had to wait many hours. It was not until nearly four o'clock in the afternoon that a dull roar proceeding from the throng on the Pont Notre-Dame announced that the gloomy cortège had set forth from the Grand Châtelet.

The previous tedium was then forgotten, and all eyes were turned towards the bridge, over which a large body of archers, numbering as many as two hundred, was presently seen to advance, but at a very slow pace. In the midst of this unusually strong escort, were two charrettes, each drawn by four horses. In the foremost of the cars, with his back to the horses, sat the Comte de Horn —a long black cloak completely shrouding his person, which had been almost stripped of its attire, in preparation for the dreadful punishment he had to undergo. The deathly pallor of his features was heightened by the sombre hue of the cloak, and his looks showed that he was appalled by the frightful yells and execrations addressed to him by the savage spectators. Once or twice he stole a glance at the crowd, but instantly averted his gaze from the fierce and pitiless looks he encountered. Nothing but abhorrence and gratified vengeance was written in the faces he beheld. He tried to pray, but his mouth was parched, and his ashy lips refused their office. His only resource was to fix his eyes steadfastly upon the crucifix held towards him by Père Gueret, who accompanied him in the charrette.

Not such was the demeanour of De Mille, who occupied the hindmost car, and was attended by the chaplain of the Châtelet. Like his wretched associate, he was wrapped in a long black cloak, but the cries by which he was assailed, so far from cowing him, roused all the fierceness of his nature, and glancing defiantly around, he requited the spectators with looks as menacing as their own. At last, stung beyond endurance at the continuous hooting, he rose from his seat, and looked as if about to fling himself, bound as he was, upon his tormentors. The chaplain, however, prevailed upon him to sit down. This display of courage operated in his favour with the mob, and their invectives lessened in fury. After this, De Mille became perfectly cool and collected, and scrutinised the spectators on either side as if in search of some familiar face. But he perceived none that was known to him, until just as he reached the foot of the bridge his eye alighted upon the two Irishmen. Reproaching himself for the wrong he had done them, he turned away, and was instantly engrossed by other objects.

By this time, the car containing the Comte de Horn had entered the Place de Grève, and a frightful yell arose from the assemblage. This ordeal was perhaps the most terrible that the wretched young man had to endure, and he internally prayed for deliverance. So dense was the crowd, that it was with difficulty that a passage could be forced through it by the archers, and two or three stoppages occurred in consequence. During these unavoidable delays the Comte de Horn suffered indescribable anguish, so that before he reached the place of execution, it might be truly said with him that the bitterness of death had almost passed.

Already half a dozen ominous-looking personages, clad in habiliments of blood-red serge, and having their muscular arms bared to the shoulder, had taken possession of the scaffold, and from that eminence were watching the slow progress of the charrettes through the concourse. These were the two executioners and their aids.

So faint was the Comte de Horn, that, on reaching the spot where he was about to expiate his offences with his life, he had to be helped out of the car, and could not mount the scaffold without assistance. On gaining the summit and beholding the horrible apparatus prepared for him, he would have sunk, if the assistants had not quickly placed him in a chair.

But De Mille maintained an undaunted deportment to the last. Although he was still very lame from the effects of his fall from the window of the Epée de Bois, he refused all assistance to ascend the steps of the scaffold. As he reached the fatal platform, the yells that were resounding on all sides suddenly ceased, and a deep silence ensued. Amid this hush, which was the more impressive from the contrast it offered to the previous din, De Mille took a last look around.

With a composure which, under the circumstances, was astonishing, and which extorted something of admiration from the thousands who watched him, he allowed his gaze to wander over the sea of upturned faces that invaded the scaffold on all sides—noted the old and picturesque habitations forming one side of the Place de Grève—surveyed the stately Hôtel de Ville, and remarked the line of carriages drawn up before it, wondering how they came to be there; and then, bidding an everlasting adieu to all on earth, cast a look towards heaven, and was still gazing upwards, when a slight touch on the shoulder recalled him to the terrible business on hand. He then perceived that De Horn was kneeling before the curé of Saint Paul, and immediately prostrated himself beside him.

During all this time the crowd kept such profound silence that the voices of the prisoners reciting their prayers could be distinctly heard at some distance from the scaffold. Their devotions over, Père Gueret exhorted them to bear their sufferings with resignation, and to trust in the

Saviour who had died for them. He then held the crucifix to their lips, and they both kissed it fervently.

Hitherto, no word had passed between them since they quitted the Châtelet, and they had not even exchanged a look. Had it been possible, De Mille would have embraced his unhappy associate, but his arms being bound, he could only gaze mournfully into his face.

"Comte de Horn," he said, "I implore your forgiveness. If you had not listened to my evil suggestions your hands would be free from blood, and you would not be upon this scaffold. I am the author and instigator of the crime for which we are both about to suffer. On my head alone ought to fall the punishment. My sole concern is that you must share my doom. Can you forgive me?"

"I do—I forgive you as I hope myself to be forgiven," replied De Horn, earnestly. "It matters little who suggested the crime. Our guilt is equal. May Heaven have mercy upon us both!"

"Amen!" ejaculated De Mille, fervently.

"Are you ready?" demanded the principal executioner, in a harsh voice.

Both prisoners replied in the affirmative.

"Heaven support you!" cried Père Gueret and the chaplain together. "We will pray for you."

The prisoners were then divested of their cloaks, and each was taken to the wheel intended for him, and bound tightly to it by cords.*

During this terrible process, the Comte de Horn uttered many woful ejaculations, but his companion set his teeth firmly, and did not allow a word or groan to escape him.

When the assistants had completed their task, the executioners, each wielding a heavy bar of iron, advanced towards them.

At this moment a perceptible shudder ran through the assemblage, and shrieks and stifled exclamations were heard.

De Horn closed his eyes, and called upon all

the saints for succour, but De Mille spoke not, and fixed such a look upon the executioner who approached him, as almost to intimidate the wretch.

It is not our design to inflict upon our readers any description of the dreadful scene that ensued. Happily, the horrible punishment to which the unhappy young men were subjected, and which was first practised in Paris during the reign of the chivalrous Francis the First, has long been abolished. But we may mention, in order to show the severity of the torture, that a coup de grace was never given to the sufferer. In the case before us, it is upon record that after the executioner had done his butcherly work upon the Comte de Horn, and broken his comely limbs, the miserable young man was allowed to remain in his agony for an hour and a half before death relieved him.

De Mille escaped with much less suffering. One of the assistants, who had been paid for the service, allowed the end of the rope that bound the culprit's neck to the wheel to drop between the planks. This cord was seized by a hand beneath and tightened, so that De Mille was strangled almost before the executioner began his work.

The hand that pulled the cord and thus relieved the wretched young man from further torture was that of old Delmace.

The Regent having adjudged the confiscation of the property of the unhappy Comte de Horn to his brother Prince Maximilien, received the following scornful letter:

"I do not complain, monseigneur, of the death of my brother. But I do complain that your royal highness has violated in your own person the rights of the nobility and of the nation. I thank you for the confiscation of my brother's goods, but I should deem myself as infamous as he was if I received any favour from you. May God and the king one day render you justice as strict as you have rendered my unhappy brother!"

End of the Seventh Book.

BOOK VIII.

THE DOWNFAL OF THE SYSTEM.

I.

HOW THE MISSISSIPPIANS WERE DRIVEN FROM THE RUE QUINCAMPOIX.

THE dreadful crime perpetrated by the Comte de Horn and his associates furnished Law with a pretext for suppressing all agiotage, which, owing to the manœuvres of the Mississippians, who had now begun to speculate on the baisse, had become so prejudicial to the System. Accordingly, he issued a decree, prohibiting all persons from assembling in the Rue Quincampoix for the purpose of dealing in shares. The decree likewise prohibited any banker or broker from keeping a bureau in the street.

On the publication of this edict, the Mississippians, who began to assemble as usual in the Rue Quincampoix, were driven out by the guard; all the bureaux were closed; and the street, lately the busiest and noisiest in Paris, became silent and deserted.

Law, however, found it utterly impossible to extinguish the fire which he himself had kindled. The passion for gambling still burnt as fiercely as ever in the breasts of the speculators. Expelled from their favourite rendezvous, the Mississippians met in detached groups in the Place des Victoires, in the Rue de la Ferronnerie, on the quays, and in other places, and though constantly dispersed by patrols, they managed to conduct their operations as before.

Thus baffled, Law issued a still more stringent decree, prohibiting all meetings for stock-jobbing purposes in any place whatsoever, on pain of imprisonment, and a fine of three thousand livres. But this second decree was violated in the same flagrant manner as the first, and determined resistance being offered by the Mississippians to those who interfered with them, Law at last very reluctantly agreed to allow them a legitimate place of meeting in the Place Vendôme.

Very different was the aspect of this new mart from that of the Rue Quincampoix, and the Mississippians gained immensely in comfort and convenience by the exchange from a narrow crowded street to a broad open place. Tents, ranged in lines across the magnificent area of the Place Vendôme, produced a novel and charming effect, and delighted the pleasure-loving Parisians, who flocked thither in crowds, as to a fair. Half of the tents were occupied by bankers and brokers from the Rue Quincampoix; the other half, which comprised the largest and most elegant of these temporary structures, were tenanted by traiteurs and dealers in costly stuffs, jewellery, and ornaments of all kinds.

Though the assemblage in the Place Vendôme

was under the surveillance of the police, yet as a vast number of disorderly persons of both sexes mixed with it, the scenes that frequently took place caused so much scandal, that Law broke up the camp, and transferred the Mississippians to another locality.

It may be remembered that among Law's vast possessions was the Hôtel de Soissons, which he had purchased for a very large sum from the Prince de Carignan. In the garden attached to this hotel he caused six hundred barraques to be constructed, and these he let at a very high rent to the bankers and brokers, the traiteurs, cafetièrs, cabaretiers, gambling-house keepers, and the various traders who ministered to the wants and pleasures of the Mississippians.

"The garden of the Hôtel de Soissons does not contain more than a couple of acres," writes Duhautchamp, "but there is not any other piece of ground in France of the same size which could produce so high a rent, since each barraque was let for five hundred livres a month, and the annual revenue would have amounted to three millions six hundred thousand livres if the garden had not proved the tomb of the System. The lines of barraques formed streets, which were paved, and in the midst there was a fountain, always gushing with water. The trees which were allowed to remain gave the place the appearance of the fair of Saint Laurent. There was no sort of traffic that did not take place in this garden. Gold itself was sold by the marc, the price being regulated by a manœuvre corresponding with that adopted in regard to paper. There were money-changers who cashed by the day a certain quantity of billets de banque to amuse the lower classes. Jewels, which six months before the opening of the gardens had cost only a hundred pistoles in billets de banque, were now resold for seven or eight thousand livres in the same paper; so that those who disposed of them made very considerable gains. Goods and apparel of all kinds were brought to the garden as to a market; but persons without occupation and of bad character, resorting to the taverns and cafés, threw the place into confusion."

II.

THE FATAL EDICT.

DURING all this time Law's efforts to uphold the System had been incessant but ineffectual. Decree after decree was issued, but with no other result than to aggravate the difficulties of the position. Specie was almost entirely banished, but though the billets de banque maintained their nominal value, the price of provisions and of all other necessaries was trebled, so that in effect the notes were depreciated to that extent. The shares of the Compagnie des Indes, which was now united to the Bank, had undergone a rapid and continuous fall, and were now not worth a twentieth part of the price to which they had been raised by the manœuvres of the Realisers. Moreover, there was every prospect that they would sink still lower, while it appeared equally certain that the billets de banque must be further depreciated.

Evidently a terrible financial crisis was at hand. No sooner did this become clear, than Law at once lost the wonderful popularity he had enjoyed. From being proclaimed on all hands, as we have seen from the ovation offered him in the Rue Quincampoix, as the regenerator and saviour of the country, he was now denounced as its worst enemy. The courtiers, whom he had enriched, caballed against him, and endeavoured to procure his overthrow. His mortal enemy, D'Argenson, who still retained the office of keeper of the seals, was most active in these plots; and, worse than all, the Abbé Dubois, who had hitherto been his staunch ally, turned against him. All the Regent's

Roués were anxious for his dismissal from office, and Nocé, who, as we know, piqued himself upon his skill as a physiognomist, predicted that the comptroller-general would die by the rope. The Regent, however, who had a sincere regard for Law, refused to listen to the suggestions of his enemies.

At last, however, D'Argenson and Dubois resolved to bring matters to an issue, and in a conference which they had with the Regent, endeavoured to open his eyes to the peril in which the country was placed by the extension given to the System.

"Up to the present date," said D'Argenson, "billets de banque have been issued to the extent of two thousand six hundred millions, whereas the whole specie of the kingdom amounts only to thirteen hundred millions. To save the country from ruin, it is absolutely necessary that the proportion should be equalised between the notes and the coin, and this can only be done by doubling the value of the latter, which, I own, would be an extremely hazardous experiment, or by reducing the value of the notes to one-half."

"I am in favour of the latter expedient," said the Abbé Dubois. "It is impossible the notes can be repurchased by the government, and consequently there is no alternative but to reduce them."

"The proposition I would submit to your highness is this," pursued D'Argenson, "that the shares of the Compagnie des Indes be gradually reduced from their present price of eight thousand livres to five thousand, when they shall remain fixed and unalterable. I also propose that the billets de banque be reduced in a similar manner—for example, that a note of ten thousand livres be reduced at the rate of five hundred livres a month, until it declines to five thousand, or one-half its present value, when it shall remain fixed. The lesser notes, of course, to be reduced in the same proportion."

"The plan merits consideration," said the Regent.

"Every consideration has been given to it by the Duc de la Force, the Duc d'Antin, and myself, and we are agreed that it is the only means of averting a crisis," said D'Argenson. "The public interests imperatively demand that the step should be taken, and I urge upon your highness the necessity of issuing an edict to that effect without delay."

At this moment Law entered the cabinet, when the Regent acquainted him with the proposition which had just been made by D'Argenson, and asked his opinion of it.

"I condemn it in the strongest terms possible," replied Law, indignantly regarding D'Argenson. "It is a most impolitic measure, and will prove destructive alike to the System and the country. If the System be allowed to go on in the way I have planned, though it may be beset with difficulties at the present moment, it must prosper. The annual revenue of the Compagnie des Indies is above eighty millions, and is susceptible of great increase. We can make good all our engagements, and pay a dividend of two hundred livres on each share that has been created. Our credit is unlimited. Our funds are enormous. We have the whole foreign trade, and all the public revenues of the kingdom, in our hands. We enjoy the protection of the government, and the confidence of the people. What, then, is there to fear?"

"The collapse of the System," replied D'Argenson. "But I deny that you possess the confidence of the people, or that the government can protect you. Your shares are daily declining, and your notes are depreciated. The Bank is almost drained of specie, so that if there should be a run upon it, it must infallibly stop payment, and a national bankruptcy ensue."

"I am under no apprehension of such an emergency," replied Law. "The issue of the notes has been greater than was originally intended, but the number was increased in order to pay off the State debts, and this being accomplished, the notes, as they are paid in, will be destroyed."

"But that process is too slow," said D'Argenson. "The danger is imminent. A remedy the most energetic and the most efficacious must be found, and that I have proposed to his highness."

"What you propose will be the death-blow of the System, and that you design," rejoined Law. "His highness, I trust, will reject your perfidious proposition. By the course proposed confidence will be for ever destroyed, and with the loss of confidence the System, which is sustained by credit, must inevitably fall."

"You must yield to necessity," rejoined D'Argenson. "The inordinate development you have given to your System has brought you to this pass."

"Have I done nothing with the System?"

said Law. "Have I not paid the State the fifteen hundred millions I engaged to furnish to it? Have I not rendered numerous services to the kingdom? Have I not introduced order into its finances? Have I not colonised the Mississippi, built two new cities, and created a foreign commerce? Have I not improved agriculture as well as trade? Have I not raised the price of the land, so as to enable the noble to pay off his encumbrances, and have I not given work to the artisan?"

"All this you have done," replied D'Argenson. "But your System has brought the country to the verge of bankruptcy, and it is for us to save it, and to save you, from the consequences of your rashness. Therefore we urge this measure upon his Highness the Regent."

"I vehemently protest against it," said Law, "and I repeat that the measure will produce the very evils you propose to remedy. Do not gratify the malice of my enemies, monseigneur," he added to the Regent. "They are seeking only my ruin in the perfidious advice they give you. They care not if they bring destruction upon the country, provided they get rid of me. Rather than this fatal decree should be issued, I will retire from office."

"No, no, that must not be," said the Regent. "But I confess I do not think the measure so perilous as you represent it."

"It is absolutely necessary," said D'Argenson. "M. Law cannot be a judge in his own case. His reliance upon the System blinds him to the danger by which he is menaced."

"Well, I will issue the edict, and take all the responsibility of it upon myself," said the Regent.

"That will not relieve me, monseigneur," said Law. "All the consequences of this impolitic, this unjust measure, will fall on my head. I shall be charged with defrauding the holders of notes of half their money. If my services have earned any gratitude from your highness, I pray you manifest it now. Out of consideration for me, do not take this step, which must destroy me."

"Do not yield, monseigneur," whispered Dubois, drawning close to the Regent. "He has not assigned his true reasons for opposing the edict. I will explain them anon. Be firm."

"Your answer, monseigneur?—your answer?" cried Law.

"The edict will be issued," rejoined the Regent.

Law did not attempt further remonstrance, but made an obeisance, and quitted the cabinet.

"We have gained our point," observed D'Argenson to Dubois. "I have requited him for the injury he did me."

"And I have removed a formidable rival," returned Dubois.

The consequences predicted by Law followed the publication of the fatal edict. By this thunderstroke, the fabric which he had created with so much pains fell to the ground.

All classes of society were seized with consternation, and, as soon as they recovered from the shock, vented their anger in loud reproaches against Law, whom they regarded as the author of the decree. Mobs assembled in different quarters, and so violently excited was the public mind, that it was deemed necessary to call out the troops to prevent an insurrection.

Ever inimical to Law, the parliament, espoused the public opinion, and declaimed against the decree as unjust and iniquitous. The nobles were equally indignant, and the Duc de Bourbon, who lost half his immense gains, came in a state of fury to the Regent, and could not be appeased except by four millions.

Far from abating, however, the popular irritation increased, and the animosity to Law became so universal that his life was not considered safe. Seditious and inflammatory placards were posted on the walls, and amongst these were these lines, conveying a threat both to Law and the Regent:

Jean Law a merité la corde,
Et le Régent le coutelas ;
Et voilà d'où vient la concorde
De notre Régent avec Lass.*

Moreover, warning letters were sent to several householders, couched in these terms: "You are warned that, unless affairs change their aspect, there will be another Saint-Bartholomew on Saturday next. Do not, therefore, go out on that day if you value your life. Heaven preserve you from fire!"

Yet even at this period the Parisians jested at their misfortunes, and this song was chanted to the appropriate air *des Pendus*:

Lundi, j'achetai des actions,
Mardi, je gagnais des millions,
Mercredi, j'ornai mon ménage,
Jeudi, je pris un équipage,
Vendredi, je m'en fus au bal,
Et Samedi a l'hôpital.

* The financier's name was thus pronounced by the Parisians.

III.

AN ÉMEUTE.

SIX days after the promulgation of the fatal decree another edict was issued by the Regent restoring the actions and notes to their former value. But it was now too late. Confidence was gone. Credit had been annihilated by the first blow, and the mischief was found to be irreparable. The only effect of the new edict was to enable unprincipled persons to compel their creditors to take the discredited notes. To increase the disastrous state of things, payment was stopped at the Bank, under the pretext that great frauds had been committed by some of the clerks, and that it was necessary to examine the accounts. This was done to prevent the further drain of specie. The prohibition against the possession of gold was withdrawn, but the favour was treated with derision, since it came at a moment when all gold was gone.

The distress of the people now became intolerable, and it seemed probable that thousands, possessed of paper-money, which now became worthless, would perish from starvation. Workmen were at once thrown out of employment; manufactures and commerce came to a stand,—not only in Paris, but in the provinces, dividends, wages, and pensions were no longer paid—in short, the public ruin was complete. The State finances were no better. The treasury was emptied, and the king himself without a revenue.

In resuming its payments, which it did after a few days' closure, the Bank at first only cashed notes of a hundred livres, and shortly afterwards only those of ten livres. The workmen, the small shopkeepers, and all those whose small means scarcely sufficed for existence, besieged the Hôtel Mazarin night and day, and filled the Rue Vivienne and the Rue Neuve des Petits Champs with a compact mass. The crowd was as great as that collected on the same spot to obtain subscriptions, but the motive that brought them there was widely different. Many persons passed the entire night at the gates of the Hôtel Mazarin. When the gates were opened the rush was terrible, and scarcely a day passed that several persons were not stifled or trampled under foot.

"To arrive at the bureaux," says the chronicler of the Journal de la Régence, "it was necessary to pass between a long wooden barricade, on the top of which workmen and porters clambered, and flung themselves upon the crowd, increasing the pressure, and throwing down many, who were trampled under foot, and much injured. Such was the eagerness to obtain a miserable pistole at the peril of life and limb. From three o'clock in the morning the Rue Vivienne was filled from one extremity to the other with a crowd collected from all the quarters in the city and the remotest faubourgs, in order to be first to enter the garden-gate of the Hôtel Mazarin, when it should please the directors of the Compagnie des Indes and the clerks to show themselves at the bureaux in the gallery to make payments, which rarely commenced before eight or nine o'clock, and continued till noon, or perhaps an hour later. On leaving the gallery, all those who had secured a pistole hurried to a tavern to refresh themselves after their frightful fatigue. A number of persons scaling the ruins of the houses which Law had begun to pull down in the Rue Vivienne, ran along the garden-wall of the Hôtel Mazarin, and catching hold of the branches of the chesnut-trees planted near the wall, let themselves drop into the garden, there to await the opening of the barricade some three or four hours later."

Sometimes all this patience was expended in vain, and the bureaux were inexorably closed. Then arose complaints and maledictions against Law and the Regent; stones and other missiles were hurled against the windows of the Hôtel Mazarin; and these disorderly proceedings irritating the guard, sanguinary collisions would ensue. On one occasion, the angry crowd having thrown stones at the windows, as before mentioned, twenty soldiers of the Invalides dispersed them at the point of the bayonet, wounding and arresting several.

A deplorable incident, which occurred at this time, had well-nigh caused Paris to be delivered up to the fury of the famished and justly-incensed mob.

One night a greater concourse than usual encumbered the Rue Vivienne and the Rue Neuve des Petits-Champs. More than fifteen thousand persons, densely packed together, impatiently awaited the opening of the bureaux. A tumult arose, owing to the terrible pressure of those in the rear of the throng. Cries and groans proclaimed that numbers were injured, and when day dawned fifteen mutilated corpses were picked from beneath the feet of the crowd.

At this frightful spectacle the concourse, roused to fury, and forgetting the object that had brought them thither, abandoned the Bank, and shouting vengeance against Law and the Regent, placed the bodies on litters, five of which were borne to the Place Vendôme, and set down before the Hôtel Law. They then commenced an attack upon the house, declaring they would hang the comptroller-general; but before they could break open the gates a detachment of the Swiss guard appeared, and drove them away.

Meantime, all the approaches to the Palais were beset, the infuriated crowd demanding the Regent with loud cries. They were told he was at Bagnolet, but the assurance was disbelieved, and the vociferations increasing in violence, reached the chamber of the prince, and aroused him.

At the peril of his life, M. le Blanc, minister of war, descended amongst the crowd, distributed money amongst them, and sought to calm them. It being above all things necessary to get rid of the bodies, the sight of which inflamed the popular indignation, Le Blanc selected some half-dozen persons who appeared leaders of the outbreak, and said to them,

"My friends, remove these bodies. Deposit them in a church, and return to be paid."

The coolness of the minister and the promise of the reward produced the desired effect. He was obeyed. This diversion afforded time to introduce disguised mousquetaires into the palace; the royal guard had been despatched from the Tuileries; and the lieutenant-general of police had arrived with two brigades of the watch. The Regent was out of danger, and the gates of the palace were thrown open.

IV.

HOW LAW'S CARRIAGE WAS DEMOLISHED.

BEING informed that the tumult had in a great degree subsided, about an hour before noon Law entered his carriage, and drove to the Palais Royal. As he was passing along the Rue Saint Honoré, his carriage was recognised by a number of riotous persons, who still beset the neighbourhood of the Palais Royal, and was instantly surrounded and stopped.

A woman, whose husband had been crushed to death in the tumult at the gates of the Hôtel Mazarin, advanced to the door of the carriage, and shaking her clenched hands in his face, exclaimed:

"Robber and murderer! if there were only four women like me, you should be torn in pieces!"

This exclamation might have roused the passions of the crowd, if two men, whom Law recognised as the Irishmen, had not seized hold of the woman and dragged her forcibly away.

Taking advantage of the interference, Law, who had not for a moment lost his self-possession, leaped out of the carriage, and eyeing the angry crowd with contempt, called out, "Arrière! vous êtes des canailles."

Overawed by his looks and deportment, those nearest him drew back, while the two Irishmen, having returned, stood beside him, ready to defend him from attack.

With a grateful glance at the devoted fellows, Law regained the carriage, the door of which was closed by Terry, and in another moment Law had passed safely through the gates of the Palais Royal.

On its return the empty carriage was again stopped by the mob, when the coachman, André, had the imprudence to imitate his master, and adopting the same language, called out, "A-bas! vous êtès des canailles!" Like success, however, did not attend him. No sooner were the words uttered than he was pulled from the box, assailed by a hundred furious hands, and carried away half dead. The carriage was demolished.

On the same morning the Court of Parliament had assembled to deliberate upon the grave events which had just occurred, and a debate was going on, when the president, M. de Mesmes, who had just received intelligence of the destruction of Law's carriage, called out,

> Messieurs, messieurs, bonne nouvelle!
> Le carosse de Law est réduit en caunelle.

The news was welcomed by loud plaudits from

the whole court, and a voice inquired, "Is Law also torn in pieces?"

"I am sorry I cannot give you that satisfactory piece of intelligence," replied the president.

"Then we will issue a décret de prise-de-corps against him," cried several voices.

V.

HOW THE PARLIAMENT WAS EXILED TO PONTOISE.

On entering the Palais Royal, Law found the vestibule and gallery full of soldiers. In the Regent's cabinet were assembled the Duc de Bourbon, the Duc D'Antin, the Duc de la Force, Dubois, and D'Argenson. The events of the morning had greatly excited the Regent, the alarm he had at first experienced having given way to rage. Far from endeavouring to calm his anger, Dubois and D'Argenson heightened it by their observations. The prince was pacing to and fro within the chamber, but when Law made his appearance he rushed up to him, and in a voice hoarse from excess of passion, cried out, "Ha, traitor! ha, villain! Do you know what you have done? You have caused the death of twenty persons, and have spread sedition and discontent throughout Paris. The king himself is not safe. You have placed us all in peril. The people demand your head, and I do not see why I should refuse to gratify their just desire for vengeance."

"Deliver me up to them, if you think fit, monseigneur," replied Law. "Order my instant execution if you will, but do not charge me with offences I have not committed. I am not the author of the calamities which have just occurred, and which I profoundly regret. On the contrary, if my advice had been listened to—if the fatal edict, which I strenuously opposed, had not been issued—this dire misfortune would have been prevented. The real author of the mischief is M. D'Argenson, and your anger ought to be visited on him, and not on me. It was his aim to crush the System, and he has succeeded. But in executing his criminal and vindictive design, he has jeopardised the safety of your highness, and well-nigh caused a revolution."

"M. Law asserts the truth," said the Duc de Bourbon. "This popular ferment has been entirely caused by that baneful edict. If any one is sent to the Bastille—if any one is put to death—it ought to be D'Argenson. I myself am a sufferer by his infamous machinations."

"I have no desire to leave you, monseigneur, at a perilous conjuncture like the present," said Law; "but I cannot consent to sit in the same council with M. D'Argenson. Either he or I must retire."

"Your highness cannot hesitate for a moment in the selection," remarked Dubois.

"I should think not," observed the Duc de Bourbon, dryly.

"No; I cannot part with M. Law," cried the Regent. "Therefore you must resign the seals, sir," he added to D'Argenson, "and D'Aguesseau shall be recalled from exile."

"Is a minister who has served you only too zealously, monseigneur, to be thus summarily dismissed?" interposed Dubois.

"Do not intercede for me," said D'Argenson. "M. Law has regained his ascendancy, and my disgrace naturally follows; but his highness will soon find out that he has preferred a mischievous counsellor to a faithful servant."

With this he made a profound obeisance to the Regent, and, casting a vindictive glance at Law, quitted the cabinet.

Shortly afterwards, M. la Vrillière, secretary of state, and M. le Blanc, entered, and a long discussion took place as to the measures necessary to be taken to crush the sedition. It was agreed on all hands that the parliament, from its avowed hostility to the government, was certain to keep the fire smouldering, and possibly rouse it again into a general conflagration, and that it was therefore indispensable to avert the danger by an immediate coup d'état against that body. Scarcely had this resolution been arrived at, when an usher announced that a deputation from the Court of Parliament, headed by the president, solicited an audience.

"Admit them instantly," said the Regent. "They have come at the right moment."

The deputation being then ushered in, was very coldly received by the Regent.

"Monseigneur," said the president, "we are come in the name of the people to demand that full inquiry be made into the causes of the terrible calamity that has just occurred at the gates of the Hôtel Mazarin. We trust also that prompt measures will be taken by your highness to alleviate the general distress."

"Full investigations shall be made, rely upon it, M. le Président," replied the Regent, "and as far as possible the sufferings of the people shall be relieved. But the parliament, by its constant opposition to the government, and its refusal to register our edicts, is the primary cause of the present scarcity of specie, and I will take good care that this fact shall be generally understood."

"Your highness will find it difficult to induce the public to credit that statement," remarked the president.

"Hear me, M. le Président," said Law. "The Compagnie des Indes will engage to reimburse and extinguish fifty millions of billets de banque a month, on the condition that their commercial privileges shall be renewed in perpetuity. Will the parliament register a decree to that effect?"

"No," replied the president, decidedly. "We will not perpetuate the Company by saving the Bank. Such is the feeling of distrust we entertain of your projects, M. Law, that we will register no edict emanating from you."

"You had better think twice, messieurs, before you refuse to register this edict," said the Regent, in a menacing tone.

"It is not a question which requires deliberation, monseigneur," said the president. "The parliament will do nothing to uphold M. Law's pernicious System."

"You will do nothing to support the government," rejoined the Regent. "If you continue obstinate, I warn you that an order shall be issued for your exile to Pontoise."

The president smiled, for he did not believe in the threat.

"I think it right to inform you, monseigneur," he said, "that we have just issued a décret de prise-de-corps against M. Law, and are determined to bring him to trial."

"Then you must execute the writ in this palace, for here he will remain," replied the Regent. "You have heard my resolve. If you continue contumacious, you go to Pontoise. Adieu, messieurs."

The audience being thus terminated, the deputation withdrew.

The parliament did not believe that the Regent,

in the present temper of the people, would dare to execute his threat. They therefore brought matters to a speedy issue by peremptorily refusing to register the decree proposed by Law. Upon this, the Palais de Justice was at once invested by troops, and mousquetaires were sent to conduct the president and counsellors of parliament to Pontoise.

This coup d'état caused great amusement at court, and gave rise to the following lampoon, at which the Regent laughed heartily:

Le parlement est à Pontoise
    Sur Oise,
Par ordre du Régent.
Mais nous rendra-t-on notre argent ?
Non !—c'est pour chercher noise
    Au parlement,
Qui s'en va coucher à Pontoise
    Sur Oise,
Par ordre du Régent.

Notwithstanding all the expedients resorted to, the financial crisis increased daily in severity. The prices of provisions and of all articles, which could only be purchased by discredited notes, became so excessive as to be wholly out of the reach of the poor, many of whom died of absolute famine, and citizens lately wealthy and prosperous sank into poverty. As the high prices were continually increasing while the notes diminished in value, it will be easily imagined by what feelings of rage and despair the bulk of the community were agitated. Threats the most terrible were again uttered against Law and the Regent, and if they had not both been attended by a strong escort, it is certain that violent hands would have been laid upon them.

The Princess Palatine mentions in her Memoirs, that at this period she received numerous letters containing frightful threats against the Regent. In one of the letters she was informed that two hundred bottles of poisoned wine had been prepared for her son, and it was added, if these failed, that a new kind of fire would be employed to burn him alive in the Palais Royal.

Menaces equally terrible were addressed to Law.

No epithet was too injurious to be levelled against him, and the mildest form of expression was "Gueux infame! fripon! scélérat!" As he had lately been the idol of the people, so now he had become the object of their greatest detestation.

Notwithstanding the popular clamour, however, the Regent would not give him up, and fresh placards were posted on the walls, to this effect: "Save the king! Kill the Regent! Hang Law! and brave the consequences!" The populace also were excited to outrage and plunder by incendiary songs like the following, which were heard in all the cabarets:

> Français, la bravoure vous manque!
> Vous êtes plein d'aveuglement.
> Pendre Law avec le Régent,
> Et vous emparer de la Banque,
> C'est l'affaire d'un moment.

And another, equally menacing, which commenced thus:

Français, garde ton argent,
Laisse dire le Régent.
Le fripon de Law va être pendu!

What would have been Law's fate, if he had fallen into the hands of the infuriated populace at this juncture, was made manifest by the narrow escape of M. Boursel. This gentleman was passing in his carriage along the Rue Saint Antoine, when his course was obstructed by a fiacre, the driver of which refusing to move, M. Boursel's lacquey immediately got down, and, seizing the horse's head, tried to drag him out of the way. On this, the hackney-coachman immediately shouted out, "I see who is in the carriage! it is the robber Law. Friends!" he added, vociferating still more loudly, "Here is Law! Kill him! kill him!"

On hearing these cries, the people rushed instantly towards the carriage, and would, no doubt, have torn the unfortunate gentleman in pieces, if he had not managed to escape into the church of the Grands Jésuites. But even here he would not have found a sanctuary, for he was pursued as far as the high altar, if a small door had not afforded him a means of exit into the convent, where he was safe.

VI.

THE CONVENT OF THE CAPUCINES.

After the death of her father, Colombe remained for a few weeks in perfect seclusion at Guermande. She then announced her intention of retiring for ever from the world, and burying her sorrows in a convent. Vainly did Lady Catherine Law use every argument to dissuade her from the step. Vainly did little Kate add her entreaties to those of her mother. Vainly did Evelyn implore her not to abandon him—nothing could change her resolution.

"What have I to live for?" she said to Evelyn.

"I will not bring shame and dishonour on those I have loved. When that dreadful catastrophe, which has darkened my life, occurred, I felt that all my hopes of earthly happiness were over. I shall never cease to love you, Evelyn, but I cannot now be your wife."

"Why not?" cried Evelyn, distractedly. "No opprobrium can attach to you."

"The world will think differently, Evelyn," she rejoined. "A stigma is for ever fixed upon me, which nothing can efface. Is the sister of the unhappy Comte de Horn more guilty than I am? Was she implicated in his dreadful crime? No! Yet by his felon death she has been rendered infamous, and cannot become a canoness."

"But this unjust and cruel law only prevails in Germany, and does not exist in France. I repeat, that no obloquy can attach to you. Besides, few know that De Mille was your brother—and those who do, deeply commiserate you."

"Were the terrible truth absolutely unknown,

I could not hide it from myself," replied Colombe. "But it cannot be hidden. It will rise up against me. Were I to yield to your entreaties—were I to consent to become your wife—you would one day hate me."

"I hate you, Colombe! Impossible! Banish the notion from your mind."

"I cannot banish it. What would you say if you heard me called the sister of an assassin? No, no—Evelyn, I can never be yours. You must return to England. You must forget me. You must seek another wife. You will never find one who will love you more truly than I have done—but at least she will be free from the dreadful stigma that attaches to me."

"If I lose you I will wed no other," cried Evelyn. "But you will not leave me thus! You will not condemn me to wretchedness."

"Evelyn," she replied, sadly but firmly, "I repeat, that my decision is taken. Nothing can change it. The very love I feel for you makes me resolute. I am for ever blighted—for ever! I doubt not that you will feel the shock severely at first—but it will wear out in time."

A few days after this, Colombe entered the convent of the Capucines, in the Rue Saint Honoré. Ere she had been long an inmate of this religious house, her health began sensibly to decline, and though she made no complaint, Lady Catherine, who visited her almost daily, insisted upon sending Doctor Chirac to her, and he at once pronounced that consumption had set in, and that the insidious disease had already made too much progress to be arrested.

This terrible announcement, which filled all those who loved her with dismay, was received almost with joy by Colombe. She had prayed that a term might be put to her sufferings, and her prayers were heard. Fain would Lady Catherine, who felt for her all a mother's tender love and anxiety, have had her return to the Hôtel Law, but she could not be prevailed upon to leave the convent.

"I cannot return to the scene of my former happiness," she said. "I will die here."

A few days after this the popular disturbances broke out, and Lady Catherine then felt that it was better the poor sufferer had not been induced to quit her retreat.

But how fared it with Evelyn during this trying time? Though Colombe again and again entreated him to return to England, and though both Lady Catherine and Belinda seconded her entreaties, he refused compliance. He could not tear himself from Paris. He wandered about seeking distraction, but could never banish his gloomy thoughts. When the Place Vendôme was converted into a camp, as we have described, he went there often, noting the follies and excesses of the Mississippians with a jaundiced eye; and when the stock-jobbers were transferred to the gardens of the Hôtel de Soissons, he followed them thither, and witnessed many a singular scene—especially after the publication of the fatal edict that destroyed the System.

In the same vain search of distraction he also visited the places of public amusement, and the feelings of misanthrophy which were creeping over him were heightened by finding that when universal misery prevailed, the theatres and ball-rooms were nightly crowded. While the people were starving, the upper classes and the wealthy Mississippians were rioting in luxury. Masked balls were constantly given at the Opera, and the receipts of the house were doubled. "I have been to the theatre in the Palais Royal," writes Mathieu Marais, in his journal kept at the period, "where Baron played the Earl of Essex. The crowd was prodigious, in spite of the general distress. The women were covered with precious stones; the men magnificently attired. On one side sat the Regent with Madame de Parabère;

on the other was M. le Duc with Madame de Prie. Any one who had only seen the inside of the theatre would have thought that the kingdom was rich; but on going out the wretchedness was yet more striking by contrast." Further on the same journalist remarks: "In the midst of this misery the Opera Balls have commenced, the admission being six livres for each person. There was a great crowd on the night of Saint Martin, and many have melted away their billets de banque, sacrificing almost all they had for a dance, and leaving those at home to die of hunger. Voilà le Français, et les Parisiens!"

Such spectacles and such contrasts—misery, famine, and despair on the one hand—luxury, splendour, and profusion on the other—have never before been witnessed as were then displayed in Paris, and it was a marvel to Evelyn that the starving sufferers did not fall upon the rich and deprive them of the wealth they so ill employed.

One evening, after he had been to the garden

of the Hôtel de Soissons, Evelyn proceeded to the convent of the Capucines. For more than a week he had not been allowed admittance to Colombe, but he had learnt from the portress that she was not so well. On reaching the convent, he observed a group of persons collected before the gate, which was closed. In the midst of this group there was a miserable-looking man, who was declaiming violently against Law, taxing him with having ruined him, and evidently producing a strong effect upon his auditors. The man was still continuing his harangue, when the gates of the convent were thrown open, and a carriage came forth. But it had scarcely advanced into the street, when some one in the throng called out, "Look there! that is the livery of the robber who refuses to pay billets of ten livres."

Hearing the exclamation, the coachman applied the whip, and attempted to drive off, but the crowd were too quick for him. Regardless of the risk they incurred, several persons threw themselves in the way of the carriage, while others seized hold of the horses. Every eye was now directed to the interior of the equipage, in the hope of discovering Law. But they were disappointed. The only occupant of the carriage was a young and beautiful girl, who appeared dreadfully frightened at what was occurring. Her looks moved the crowd to compassion, and she might, perhaps, have been allowed to pass on, if the voice that had previously spoken had not called out, "It is the robber's daughter! It is Mam'zelle Law! I know her."

Immediately upon this a heavy stone was launched against the carriage-window, which Kate in her fright had drawn up, and shivered the glass. Notwithstanding the poor girl's screams, and although the blood was streaming down her face from a cut in the forehead, other missiles were thrown, and the crowd might have proceeded to yet more frightful extremities, if a deliverer had not appeared in the shape of Evelyn.

Forcing his way to the carriage, he tore open the door, and seizing Kate, who had fallen back in a half-fainting state, took her in his arms, and called out to the menacing crowd, "What! are you men, and would injure an innocent child!"

The appeal and the looks of the speaker produced the desired effect. Infuriated as they were, the crowd could not behold Kate thus presented to them and continue their violence. Those nearest to Evelyn drew back, and taking instant advantage of the movement, he flew with his burden to the convent. Already the gate had been closed by the porter, but the wicket was left open, and through this Evelyn passed, and the moment he had done so it was shut, and pursuit prevented.

On passing through the gate, Evelyn found himself in the presence of several of the nuns, who had flocked into the court-yard on hearing the disturbance. He instantly consigned poor Kate, who was still in a state of insensibility, to their charge, and she was borne off to the abbess's own room, while he himself was shown by one of the elder sisters to the parlour ordinarily allotted to visitors. Here he was left alone for some time, but at last the door opened, and the abbess entered. Her looks were so sad that Evelyn's apprehensions were roused, and he anxiously inquired how Mademoiselle Law was going on.

"She has quite recovered," replied the abbess. "No serious consequences are to be apprehended from the injury she has received. I have despatched a messenger to Lady Catherine Law to relieve her from any uneasiness in regard to her daughter. So far well. But I have sad news for you. You are aware of Colombe's precarious condition?"

"Is she worse?" cried Evelyn. "For pity's sake, tell me. Do not keep me in suspense."

"Alas! she is rapidly passing away," replied the abbess.

On hearing this, Evelyn uttered a cry of anguish so piercing that it went to the heart of his listener. She waited for a few moments till the paroxysm with which he was seized had abated, and then said, in tones of profound commiseration,

"This morning Colombe became alarmingly ill, and Doctor Chirac being hastily summoned, declared at once, on seeing her, that she had not many hours to live. As the truth could not be disguised, I was about to communicate it to the sweet sufferer, when she took my hand, and gently pressing it, said, with an angelic smile, 'I know what you are about to tell me. I could read my sentence in Doctor Chirac's looks. I feel I have not many hours to live. But death will be a relief to me, and I am fully prepared for the blow. There are two persons to whom I desire to bid farewell—Kate Law and Evelyn Harcourt.'"

An irrepressible groan burst from Evelyn.

"The request could not be refused," pursued the abbess. "Mademoiselle Law came immediately on receiving the summons, but you were not to be found, and I feared that poor Colombe's latest wish would have been ungratified, and that she would expire without beholding you. But even this disappointment, which must have been bitter to her, she bore without a murmur. But our Blessed Lady in her compassion willed it otherwise, and brought you hither for a double purpose —to be the means of rescuing Mademoiselle Law from the violence of the populace, and to soothe poor Colombe's parting pangs. You should have been admitted to her sooner, but up to this moment she has been engaged in religious offices, and could not be disturbed. Follow me, and as you value Colombe, and would not disturb her happy frame of mind, I pray you to put all possible constraint upon your feelings. This must be the condition of the interview."

They then quitted the room, ascended a staircase, and entered a gallery in which were the dormitories. Stopping at a door, the abbess softly opened it, and admitted Evelyn into a room, where he beheld a sight that well-nigh unmanned him.

On a small couch, simple in character as the rest of the furniture of the chamber, which was all of conventual plainness, lay Colombe, her appearance betokening the extremity to which she was reduced.

Approaching dissolution was written plainly on her features. Since Evelyn beheld her last, a fearful change had taken place in her countenance, but its beauty was unimpaired. So rigid were her lineaments, so like marble was their death-like hue, that she resembled an exquisite piece of monumental sculpture. Her very attitude contributed to this effect, for her thin hands pressed a crucifix devoutly to her bosom.

By the bedside knelt Kate Law, praying fervently, and at the farther end of the room were two nuns, likewise engaged in devotion. It was a profoundly touching scene, but though it afflicted Evelyn at the moment, he loved to dwell upon it afterwards, when the bitterness of his grief had passed.

The door had been opened so gently, and both the abbess and Evelyn entered with such noiseless footsteps, that at first none of the occupants of the room were conscious of their presence. The only sounds heard were the murmured prayers of Kate Law and the nuns.

Holding his breath, so as not to disturb the sacred quietude of the scene by sigh or groan, Evelyn gazed at the form of her he loved. So motionless was its attitude, that for a few moments he thought all was over, but on closer scrutiny the feeble movements caused by respiration showed that the vital spark had not yet fled. An exclamation, which he could not repress, caused Colombe to open her eyes. As she fixed them upon him, a slight, very slight, flush rose to her pallid cheeks, and a faint smile played around her lips. But the flush presently faded away, and though the eyes still rested lovingly upon him, their light grew gradually dim.

On hearing Evelyn's approach, Kate Law had risen from her kneeling posture, and moved to another part of the room.

Enabled thus to approach the dying maiden, he pressed his lips to her brow, and taking her thin cold hand, implored her to speak to him.

An effort at compliance was made by the expiring damsel. Her lips moved, but the power of articulation was gone, and no sound was audible. A very slight pressure, however, was perceptible from the hand which he grasped in his own.

To the last her gaze remained fixed upon him, and proclaimed the love which her lips were unable to utter—a love only quenched when her heart was stilled for ever.

Evelyn was roused from the stupefaction into which he was thrown, by the abbess, who said to him in a commiserating voice,

"Do not grieve for her, my son. You have only parted from her for a time. You will rejoin her in heaven. And now go hence, and leave us to pray for the soul of our departed sister."

Evelyn obeyed. Casting one last look at the inanimate body of Colombe, he quitted the chamber of death.

Before morning he was on his way to England, and not till many years afterwards did he return to Paris, when his first visit was to the chapel of the convent of the Capucines, where Colombe was interred. All her possessions had been given to the establishment.

VII.

HOW LAW RESIGNED HIS FUNCTIONS.

WITHIN twelve months from the period when the System attained its apogee, it had entirely disappeared. The billets de banque were abolished, being partially converted into rentes or actions rentières; agiotage was suppressed; the Bank shut; the shares of the Compagnie des Indes marked with discredit, and almost confiscated. The Company itself, which, according to the grand design of its founder, was to comprise the whole of the Public Revenues, the Mint, and the entire Foreign Trade with banking operations, was dismembered. This done, vigorous measures were commenced against the wealthy Mississippians, and an extraordinary commission was appointed to examine into their affairs. To prevent flight, a decree was issued prohibiting, on pain of death, any person from leaving the kingdom without a passport. These rigorous proceedings, in which he had no share, excited a fresh burst of fury against Law.

His position had, indeed, become so critical, that he could no longer hesitate to solicit his dismissal from the Regent. By arrangement, the Duc de Bourbon alone was present at the interview.

"I am come, monseigneur," said Law to the Regent, "to resign all my offices into your hands, and to request your gracious permission to quit the kingdom. I have long contemplated this step, and have only been deterred from taking it by the hope that I might be serviceable to your highness. I can now be no longer useful to you, but shall be an embarrassment rather than an assistance. The

System is entirely abolished. I have helped to undo my work, and must leave to my successors the task of reinstating the finances. Grave faults have been laid to my charge, and accusations have been brought against me, which your highness knows to be groundless. With everything at my disposal, I have profited little by the System in comparison with multitudes of others. While many have made fortunes of forty and fifty millions, I have only made twelve millions, and these have been laid out, as your highness is aware, in the purchase of lands in this country. No part of my gains have been remitted to foreign countries. That I solemnly declare."

"I entirely believe you, sir," replied the Regent, "and I beg you to understand that I have never for a moment listened to the calumnies of your enemies."

"I trust I shall not be deprived of my possessions, monseigneur," pursued Law. "When I came into this country at your highness's express invitation, I had more than two millions of livres. I owed nothing, and had large credit. In quitting France, I shall take nothing with me. I propose to cede the whole of my possessions to the Compagnie des Indes. When my debts have been paid by the Company, I will only ask that the two millions which I had when I entered into your highness's service shall be remitted to me; or that that sum shall be invested in the names of my children. I do not think this is asking too much, and I scarcely believe that my enemies will deny me justice."

"I hope this can be done, monseigneur," said the Duc de Bourbon.

"I cannot give a promise which I may be unable to fulfil," said the Regent. "If I can prevent it, your property shall not be sequestered," he added to Law.

"Hear me, monseigneur," said Law. "If I had not been charged with the general direction of the Compagnie des Indes, of the Bank, and the

Finances, and very zealous in the administration of state affairs, I should not be in my present situation; and I contend, that so far from being deprived of my possessions, if I had not the means of fulfilling my engagements, his majesty and the Company ought to furnish me with means of doing so, since I have served them with unexampled disinterestedness. But as I have effects in the hands of the Company, and other possessions, far exceeding the amount of my liabilities, it is but just that I should be allowed to settle my accounts with the Company, before any sequestration of my property shall take place."

"I have the greatest personal regard for you, M. Law, and have proved my friendship for you," replied the Regent. "If I had yielded to the solicitations of your enemies, you would be now in the Bastille. I have been given clearly to understand that your head is to be the pledge of my reconciliation with the parliament. But such a proposition, I need not say, I indignantly rejected, and only advert to it to show what my feelings are towards you. But I may not be able to prevent the confiscation of your property."

"It is for my children that I plead," said Law, in a voice of much emotion, "whose interests I have sacrificed in serving the State. If this confiscation should take place, they will be without property or home. I could have placed my daughter in the first houses of Italy, of Germany, or England, but I refused all offers, as inconsistent with my duty and attachment to the State I served. For the sake of my children—and, above all, for the sake of my daughter—I pray you, monseigneur, let not my property be wrested from me."

"Whatever may happen, you may depend upon a pension from me," said the Regent.

"After being prime minister of France, I cannot become a pensioner, monseigneur," rejoined Law, proudly.

"I trust you will not object to receive assistance

from me, M. Law," said the Duc de Bourbon. "Any sum you may require shall be at your service."

"I thank your highness," replied Law, "but I want nothing but a passport."

"That you shall have at once," replied the Regent, proceeding to his table. "Whither do you intend to proceed?"

"To Brussels, monseigneur," replied Law.

"Here is the passport," said the Regent, giving it to him. "When do you depart?"

"In a few days, monseigneur—as soon as I can arrange my affairs, and make preparations for my journey."

"Do not lose time," said the Regent. "I can no longer offer you an asylum in the Palais Royal. The parliament will return from exile to-morrow, and may cause your arrest, and then nothing can save you."

"Go to your château of Guermande to-night," said the Duc de Bourbon. "There you will be safe. Remain there till I can send my own chaise de poste to convey you to Brussels. By this plan your flight will be entirely unsuspected. Take your son with you if you choose, but leave Lady Catherine and your daughter behind. They shall be my guests at Saint Maur."

"I gratefully accept your offer, M. le Duc," replied Law, "and will follow your judicious advice. I will go to Guermande to-night, and there await the arrival of the travelling-carriage you are good enough to offer me."

"I am glad you have so decided, for I am persuaded it is the only safe course to pursue," replied the Regent. "To disarm suspicion, in case your enemies are plotting against you, you must show yourself in my box at the Opera to-night. After the performance, you can drive to Guermande. As I cannot have you at supper, you must dine with me—and you, too, M. le Duc. We may not meet again for some time," he added kindly to

Law, "and I should like to see as much of you as I can."

Thus given, the invitation could not be refused, though Law would fain have declined it.

"I see you have something further to say to me," observed the Regent to Law. "What is it?"

"Merely this, monseigneur. If I may be permitted to recommend a successor to the post I have filled in your councils, it would be M. Lepelletier de la Houssaye. He is in possession of all my views, and will be of great utility, I am sure, to your highness at this juncture."

"Have you spoken to M. de la Houssaye on the subject?" asked the Regent.

"I have, monseigneur," replied Law; "I promised to name him to your highness."

"I thought as much. He proved his gratitude by proposing to me this very morning that you should be sent to the Bastille."

"Time was when such baseness would have

stung me to the quick," said Law, "but I have experienced so much ingratitude of late, that I am become callous. I am not surprised to find M. de la Houssaye as hollow as the rest of my friends. But I adhere to the opinion I have expressed, and recommend him as the best man for the office of comptroller-general."

"He shall have the appointment," replied the Regent; "but he shall know that he owes it entirely to you, and that you asked it after being made acquainted with his perfidy."

"That is the sole revenge I desire," said Law. "When I am gone, do not forget what I have often said to you, monseigneur, that the introduction of Credit has wrought a greater change in the powers of Europe than the discovery of the Indies; that it is for the sovereign to give Credit, and not to receive it; and that the people require Credit, and must have it."

He then withdrew with the Duc de Bourbon, who conveyed him in his own carriage to the Hôtel Law.

VIII.

HOW LAW ANNOUNCED HIS DEPARTURE TO HIS FAMILY.

LAW'S ante-chambers had long since been deserted. Not one of the duchesses and other ladies of rank who had paid Lady Catherine Law so much homage now came near her, and if they met her, scarcely deigned to notice her. Their contemptible conduct, however, gave Lady Catherine little concern, and she was consoled by the friendship of Belinda, who still remained with her.

During the season of his unpopularity, Law had of course ceased to give grand entertainments, and indeed he received no company whatever; but his establishment continued the same, and was conducted on a princely scale to the last.

All his household were devoted to him, regarding him as the most generous of masters, and not one of them would leave him. Amongst the number of his dependents were our two Irish acquaintances, Terry O'Flaherty and Pat Molloy, who, after coming to his rescue when his carriage was attacked by the populace, had been taken into his service.

On his return from the Palais Royal, Law sought his wife, and found her in her boudoir with Belinda. Both being aware of his intention to resign, he at once said, "Well, it is done. The Regent has accepted my resignation. To-night I go to Guermande, where I shall remain till I start for Brussels."

"Am I not to accompany you?" said Lady Catherine.

"I wish you could," replied Law, "but it is absolutely necessary that you should remain to arrange my affairs. John will go with me, but I shall leave Kate with you, and I shall have no apprehensions whatever about you, for you will be under the care of the Duc de Bourbon. To-morrow you and Kate will go to Saint-Maur. As regards myself, I shall halt for a few days at Brussels, after which I shall make my way to Venice, where I shall take up my abode till you and Kate can join me."

"Alas!" exclaimed Lady Catherine. "Now the moment for action is come, my courage quite deserts me. You must stay with me, Belinda."

"That cannot be," said Law. "It will not be safe for you to remain in this hotel after my departure, and Belinda cannot accompany you to Saint-Maur. You must, perforce, part with her, but I hope you will soon meet again. It is impossible to say what may happen to me, or how my plans may be changed; but it is my present intention to revisit London—and at no distant date."

"You hear that, dearest Kate," cried Belinda. "Mr. Law says he will come to London, so we shall soon meet again. Nay, do not weep, my dearest friend. The trial will be hard, but you will be quite equal to it, I am sure. You have often told me how sick you are of splendour—how disgusted you are with the meanness and ingratitude of great people—and how much you long for quietude. Well, now you will have your wish, and I trust you will find that happiness in retirement which you appear to have sought in vain in the great world."

"You know I have not been happy, Belinda," rejoined Lady Catherine. "Neither do I believe there can be any real happiness amid such society as that into which I have been thrown. But I have been content to endure it, for my dear husband's sake.—You see that my words have come to pass," she added, turning to Law. "From the hour that you abjured your religion, your prosperity has deserted you."

"It would almost seem so," he rejoined, gloomily.

"Say no more on that subject now," cried Belinda. "Let me tell you my plans. To-morrow morning, when you go to Saint-Maur, Kate, I shall start for London. Luckily, my husband has a passport."

"I will ask a favour of you, Belinda, and I am sure you will grant it," cried Law. "Take those two poor Irish chairmen with you. I want to send them back to London."

"I will take them with the greatest pleasure," she replied. "Poor fellows! they have had some strange experiences of life since their arrival in Paris, and I hope will go back wiser than they came."

"Bring my children to me, Kate," said Law to his wife. "I wish to see them. Tell them what has happened."

Lady Catherine was not absent long, but reappeared with her children. Little Kate, who, like her mother and Belinda, was in mourning for Colombe, looked rather pale. She instantly flew to her father, who strained her to his breast, and kissed her tenderly.

"Your mamma has told you what has happened," he said, gazing at her with much emotion; "that I have resigned my offices to the Regent, and am about to quit Paris, in all probability for ever. My enemies have triumphed over me, and would not be content with my ruin, but would put me to death, if they got me into their hands. Therefore, I must fly to preserve my life. Come hither, John," he added to his son, "and listen to what I have to say to your sister. I hoped to make you rich, Kate, and to give you a marriage-portion equal to that of a princess. But now I have nothing to bestow upon you."

"Oh! do not think of me, dearest papa!" sobbed Kate.

"It is the thought of you and your brother that troubles me most," said her father. "Were it not for you, my darlings, I could bear my losses without a murmur."

"Do not grieve, dearest papa," said his son. "I dare say you will soon be as rich as ever again."

"I cannot indulge the hope, my dear boy," replied his father. "But I trust you may become rich by your own exertions and ability."

"Yes, I *will* become rich," cried John, emphatically. "I will try to be as great a man as you, papa."

"I trust you may be luckier than your father, John," said Law, "and not lose wealth, honour, and power, the moment you have got them in your grasp. What say you, Kate?" he added to his daughter. "Does the thought of all you have lost afflict you?"

"Not in the least, dearest papa," she rejoined. "I am only sorry for you. If you do not suffer from the change, I shall be quite content. Poor Colombe used to tell me that more real happiness is to be found in a humble abode than in a palace, and I am sure all she said was true. I shall be sorry to leave this splendid house, but wherever circumstances may take me, I shall try to be cheerful."

"And the endeavour will be crowned with success," replied her father. "But come," he added, rising. "I must take a last look at my pictures and books. My treasures will soon be dispersed, and I shall never, perhaps, behold them again."

IX.

HOW LAW TOOK A LAST SURVEY OF HIS HOUSE.

ACCOMPANIED by his two children, and followed by his wife and Belinda, he quitted the salon, and entered the grand gallery, which was crowded with antique statues and bronzes from Italy, while the walls were hung with the choicest works of the great masters. Then, passing through a noble suite of apartments, magnificently furnished in the taste of the period, he came to the library, which contained a rare collection of books, which he had purchased from the Abbé Bignon.

"I wonder into whose hands my books will

fall," thought Law, as he looked wistfully around. "Dubois has always envied me my library. I would never sell it to him. Perhaps he may get it now."

Law was right in the conjecture. After his flight, his treasures became a sort of pillage to the Regent's favourites, of which the Abbé Dubois obtained the lion's share, seizing upon the pictures, statues, and books.

It was not without a severe pang that Law quitted the library. Parting with his books was like bidding adieu to old friends, but at last he tore himself away, and proceeded to the gardens, which were laid out with great taste, and had been his especial delight, the few tranquil hours he had enjoyed since he had devoted himself to public affairs having been passed in their shady retreats. It was now December, and, consequently, the gardens were robbed of much of their attractions, but their somewhat dreary aspect harmonised better with his feelings than would have been the case if the trees had been in full foliage, and the parterres gay with flowers.

As he was retiring, he perceived the two Irishmen, who were engaged in some gardening occupations, and, calling to them, said that Mrs. Carrington was returning to London on the morrow, and had agreed to take them with her.

"But we don't want to go, do we, Pat?" rejoined Terry. "We're quite happy here, and would far rather remain with your lordship."

"Don't send us away," cried Pat. "We don't want wages—the pleasure of serving your lordship, and Lady Catherine, and mam'zelle, is enough for us."

"You must go," said Law. "I may not be able to afford you a home much longer."

"Och! that alters the question entirely," cried Terry. "We wouldn't be a burden to your lordship. But we shall be sore-hearted to laive you."

"I am quite as sorry to lose you as you can be to quit me," said Law. "Here are twenty louis d'or," he added, giving him a purse. "Divide the money between you."

"Your journey home shall be no expense to you," observed Belinda. "I and my husband will take care of you."

"Well, after all, we shall go back as rich as we cum," said Terry. "And we can always make it our boast that for a couple of months we have lived like lords, ridden in our own carriage, and kept our own valets. But wot we have best reason to be proud ov, and wot we shall nivir forget to our dyin' day, is, that we have enjoyed your lordship's notice. Be sure we shall never forget your kindness."

Bowing respectfully, they then withdrew.

X.

A GRATEFUL SERVANT.

As the party entered the house, Thierry met them, and begged to say a word to his master, upon which Law took him to his cabinet, and as soon as the door was closed, the valet said:

"I hope you will forgive what I am about to say, monseigneur. It proceeds entirely from the sincere attachment I feel for you. Situated as I am, I cannot be unaware of the difficulties in which you are placed; indeed, I can almost conjecture what will happen. Now hear me, monseigneur," he added, after a moment's hesitation.

"Owing to the position I have held in your household, and the large fees I have received, I have made a very considerable sum of money. It is to you, monseigneur, and to you alone, that I owe my fortune. Therefore it is to you that I offer it. I place the whole of it at your disposal. I trust, monseigneur, that you will honour me by accepting it. It is no gift, for the money is rightfully your own."

For a moment Law was quite overcome, and walked apart to recover himself. He then said, in a voice that betrayed his emotion, "I thank you sincerely, Thierry. You are a true friend. No man ever, perhaps, experienced such base ingratitude as I have done. Hundreds—nay, thousands—whom I have enriched have abandoned me since I have lost my credit, and so far from tendering me assistance, have conspired to hasten my ruin. Devotion like yours touches me, therefore, profoundly. I cannot accept your offer, but I fully appreciate the motives with which it is made, and am deeply sensible of your kindness."

"I fear I have not properly expressed myself, monseigneur. Do not suppose for a moment that I would presume——"

"You have displayed equal delicacy and good feeling, my good friend," interrupted Law, "and I am sure you will understand *why* I must decline your kindly offer. Nay, do not urge me more. I am not to be shaken. Neither can I allow you to follow my fallen fortunes. After the proof you have given me of your attachment, I can have no secrets from you. After the Opera to-night, I go to Guermande, where I shall remain for a day or two, and then proceed to Brussels in the Duc de Bourbon's travelling-carriage. You can go with me to Guermande, if you will, but no farther."

"I thank you for that permission, monseigneur," replied Thierry. "But I still trust you will allow me to attend you to Brussels."

"No, you must return to Paris," replied Law. "My son goes with me. Lady Catherine and my daughter will require your services, and I am sure you will oblige me by attending to them."

"On that you may rely, monseigneur."

"From motives of prudence, I shall not return to this hotel after the Opera, but shall go to the palace of the Duc de Bourbon," pursued Law. "Have the carriage there to meet me, so that I can start at once for Guermande."

"Monseigneur's directions shall be carefully obeyed. He will find the carriage waiting for him at the Palais Bourbon, and I will be with it. Can I pack up anything for monseigneur—any box or casket?"

"No," replied Law. "Of all my valuables I shall only take this ring with me. It is worth ten thousand crowns. Luckily, I have eight hundred louis d'or which were brought me this morning by M. Pomier de Saint-Léger. The money came most opportunely, for at the time I had not ten pistoles in my possession."

"Monseigneur could have had twenty thousand louis d'or, if he chose to call for them. Nay, he can have them yet."

"I thank you, my good friend. I might have been compelled to apply to you, if I had not unexpectedly received this supply from Pomier. It will amply suffice for my present requirements. And now, Thierry, you must leave me. I desire to be alone for a time."

More than an hour elapsed before Law rejoined his family, but he did not leave them again till it was time to repair to the Palais Royal. He then tenderly embraced his wife and daughter, and bade adieu to Belinda and her husband.

XI.

THE DEPARTURE.

THAT night the Opera presented a superb appearance, being filled with an extraordinarily brilliant assemblage. All the court was there. Law, who occupied a conspicuous position in the Regent's box, was an object of general curiosity, as he had not been seen in public for some time. His demeanour was marked by unusual haughtiness, and he glanced around disdainfully at the assemblage. Both the Regent and the Duc de Bourbon showed him great attention, and it was generally thought that he was completely restored to favour.

After the Opera, he proceeded to the palace of the Duc de Bourbon, where he found his carriage waiting for him, with his son and Thierry, and, entering it at once, he drove to Guermande.

Next morning Thierry returned to Paris, but came back at night with the information that Lady Catherine and her daughter had removed to the palace of the Duc de Bourbon, and that Belinda and her husband had left Paris for London, taking the two Irishmen with them.

Thierry also brought word that four of M. Law's friends and coadjutors had been arrested and sent to the Bastille—namely, M. Bourgeois, treasurer-general of the Bank; M. du Revest, comptroller of the Bank; M. Fénelon, distributor of the notes; and M. Fromaget, a director.

Alarmed by this intelligence, for he felt sure that if arrested he was lost, Law became anxious for immediate departure. He was not long detained. That night the Duc de Bourbon's equerry, M. de Sarrobert, with three confidential servants, arrived with the duke's travelling-carriage. The equerry brought a purse of gold from the duke, but Law declined it, and bidding farewell to the faithful Thierry, entered the carriage with his son. He was attended by the duke's servants, but M. de Sarrobert returned to Paris.

No interruption occurred to Law till he reached Valenciennes, when he was arrested by the intendant of Maubenge, who was no other than the son of his old enemy, D'Argenson. After a long and most vexatious detention, he was allowed to proceed to Brussels.

As soon as the arrival of the illustrious fugitive became known in that city, he was waited upon by General Wrangel, the governor, by the Marquis Pancallier, and many other important personages. A grand entertainment was given to him by the Marquis de Prie, and when he visited the theatre a vast concourse of persons assembled to behold him.

At Brussels, Law was overtaken by the envoy of

the Czar Ivan Alexiovitz, who presented him with despatches from his imperial master, praying him to take the direction of the finances. But this Law declined, and adhering to his arrangements, proceeded to Venice, where he was eventually joined by Lady Catherine and his daughter.

At first, his flight was disbelieved in Paris, but as soon as the fact was certified, this satirical piece appeared:

La chose ainsi, je monte en ma calèche,
Ça faisons dépêche;
Adieu vos écus!
Messieurs, n'y pensez plus;

Le sort m'étant favorable et propice,
Je les porte en Suisse.
Qui les reverra
Plus fin que moi sera.

Vous que l'on vit aux actions avides,
Les croyant solides,
Toujours en papier
Vouloir réaliser,

Servez vous donc de vos billets de banque;
Si l'argnet vous manque,
Cherchez le payeur
Pour avoir leur valeur.

Scarcely had the ex-minister quitted France than his possessions were sequestered by the government, under the pretext that he owed twenty millions to the Compagnie des Indes; whereas the contrary was the fact, the Company being largely indebted to him. But he could obtain no redress. He addressed several letters to the Regent, but without effect. In a letter which he sent to the Duc de Bourbon, who professed great anxiety to serve him, occurs this touching appeal: "Æsop was a model of disinterestedness. Nevertheless, the courtiers accused him of having treasures in a coffer, which he often visited. On examination, an old dress which he had worn before entering the prince's service was the only thing found. Had I but preserved my old dress, I would not change places with the wealthiest in the kingdom. But I am naked. They expect me to subsist without goods, and pay my debts without funds."

Law's System has been variously judged, but its faults have been more dwelt upon than its merits, and in the misery occasioned by its downfal, the unquestionable benefits it conferred have been forgotten. "In appreciating Law's theories," says M. Levasseur, "it must be borne in mind that he was the first to reduce into system Economical ideas. He lighted the way, and we can now, judging him and his principles with less passion than his contemporaries judged him, aver that if he was too absolute in his ideas, and too violent in his measures, he was at least animated by the desire to do good, firm in principles which he believed true, and honest in his conduct. He was useful to the science of Economy, and would have rendered great service to commerce if a prudent reserve had kept him within narrower limits."

"The conception of Law," says M. Gambier, in the "Encyclopédie de Droit," "in spite of its original errors, which rendered success impossible, in spite of the blind temerity and grave mistakes which rendered its fall so sudden and terrible, nevertheless attests in its author, in addition to a powerful and inventive genius, a distinct perception of three of the most fertile, though then unknown, sources of the greatness of nations—Maritime Commerce, Credit, and the Spirit of Association."

Financial measures infinitely more reprehensible than the System, and liable to be productive of consequences quite as disastrous, are conducted in our own day on the other side of the Atlantic; and before long we may see "greenbacks" become as worthless as Law's discredited Mississippi paper.

L'Envoy.

Our biographical romance, for such it may be termed, properly ends with Law's flight from Paris, and disappearance from public life. The rest of his history may be briefly told, since it was unmarked by any striking event. His latter days, indeed, offer a melancholy contrast to the dazzling brilliancy of his mid-career. He did not survive his disgrace many years.

While at Venice, he met Cardinal Alberoni, the exiled Spanish minister, and the Chevalier de Saint-George came from Rome to see him. The three remarkable personages had a long conference together at the convent of the Capucines.

From Venice, Law proceeded to Copenhagen, whence he sailed to England in the flag-ship of Admiral Sir John Norris, the commander of the Baltic fleet, and on arriving in London he was presented by the admiral to his Majesty King George I., and very graciously received by that monarch.

During his sojourn in London, Law fixed his abode in Conduit-street, and was visited by many persons of distinction, but his limited means compelled him to live in perfect privacy, and among the few admitted to his intimacy were Charles Carrington and Belinda. His humbler friends were not forgotten, and Terry and Pat, who had resumed their old occupation, were constantly at his door with their chair.

Sir Robert Walpole, who was very well disposed towards the fallen French minister, interested himself greatly to procure his recal by the Regent, but without effect. Failing to obtain the restitution of the property of which he had been so unjustly deprived by the French government, and finding London too expensive for him, Law at last returned to Venice, where he passed the remainder of his days.

His son, who did not survive him more than five years, died unmarried, but his daughter espoused her cousin, Viscount Wallingford.

During his retreat at Venice, Law was visited by Montesquieu, who describes him "as still the same man, his mind always occupied with projects, his head always full of calculations. Although his fortune was slender, he played constantly, and for considerable sums." Even at play he was not so lucky as heretofore, and was sometimes obliged by heavy losses to leave the sole relic of his fortunes, his valuable diamond ring, in pledge.

He died on the 21st of March, 1729, aged fifty-eight, and was buried at Venice.

His epitaph, written in Paris by a ruined Mississippian, ran thus:

Ci-gît cet Ecossais célèbre,
Ce calculateur sans égal,
Qui, par les règles de l'algèbre,
A mis la France à l'hôpital.

THE END.

CPSIA information can be obtained
at www.ICGtesting.com
Printed in the USA
LVHW101344160422
716387LV00003B/166

9 783752 594096